A Brooksville Connection

by

Jerri Drennen

Redeeming the Reporter, Book Two

Dedication

To all the women of Writers in Progress, who have been there to help me grow as a writer and have always had my back through it all.

Chapter One

Jake Mills had one shot at returning to normal life and that meant becoming someone else.

Can you meet me on Fleet Street tonight? Across from the Hawley Warehouse? Popped up in the chat box on the computer screen.

With satisfaction, he smiled and typed, *What time?*

10:00, and don't bring your cellphone.

Shit. He'd be going there with no way of signaling for help.

He blew out a ragged breath and replied. *I'll see you then.*

Jake clicked out of the site and stood, his heart rate hitching with anticipation as he glanced around the crowded public library. Once he was in Brooksville's White Nation and being indoctrinated, he'd have to stay until he learned all he could. *Danger* would be a tepid word for what he was about to tumble headfirst into, and if he got caught, he'd probably disappear. But he could see no other way. Not when all the wrong people thought he was part of the organization because of a story he'd been named in. To counter that, he'd write an exposé to prove otherwise.

He stepped out the front door of the building and into the bright sunlight, squinting as he made his way to his metallic-gray SUV. Before taking this deep nosedive into the unknown, he should stop and see his mother, let her know he wouldn't be around for a few months because of work. But she'd see straight through the ruse. Margaret Mills had a sixth sense when it came to her children, and he didn't want her to worry. He'd be better off dropping by his sister's. Silla didn't have a precognitive gift and was much too busy with her own family to pry into his plans. Yet, she'd be able to tell their mother where he was, even if it wasn't the truth. Neither needed to know the craziness he'd be walking into. They'd try and talk him out of it, and he couldn't let that happen. Returning to a decent standing with the Media was too important since it meant the difference between what he once had, job wise, and 'do you want fries with that.'

Jake cringed at the thought. He'd never pay off his student loans and return his reputation to a good place. After all, who'd want to be known as a White Supremacist? Not him. That shit followed you to the ends of the earth.

Inside his SUV, he inhaled a calming breath and turned over the engine, not at all looking forward to the forty-five-minute drive to his sister's.

He avoided a car backing out in front of him as he pulled from the library's parking lot and headed for Highway 270. He needed to play over what he'd tell his sister, just enough truth to make her believe the story. Yet not enough to have her worry about his safety. He and his sister were close, and Silla had all she needed on her plate right now.

Forty minutes later, Jake took a right into the Greenbriar subdivision and turned onto Albon St. The Cramer's lived on the roundabout at the end of the cul-de-sac in a two-story colonial, half white, half brick, new construction. He'd visited several times since his sister moved in almost a year ago and was impressed that the two could afford the home on Brian's salary. Even at the height of his career, Jake would have struggled to make the payments on the place. His brother-in-law must be doing well.

He parked and jumped out right as a bus stopped down the street and kids piled out, running in all directions, three catching Jake's eye.

"Uncle Jake," they all screamed at once, scrambling toward him, grabbing his arms and shirt, and spinning him around in a circle.

He picked up the youngest, and a few seconds later put her down. "So, how was your day at school?" he asked as they dragged him toward the front door of the house.

The oldest, in fourth grade now, made a face and said, "The same as it was yesterday. Boring."

Silla's youngest squeezed his hand and smiled up at him, causing his heart to clench. What if he never saw her again? What if he went in and they never knew what happened to him? Was he making the right decision?

"So, Uncle Jake, are you going to stay for supper? I got a new video game I want to play with you," the middle child asked, his crystal blue eyes lighting up with excitement. He was the only one of the three with Jake and his grandfather's eyes, and every time he saw the boy or looked in a mirror, he thought of his dad, gone three years now after a long battle with cancer.

He shook the thought away and grinned at his nephew. "We'll see what your mom says, okay?"

Inside the door, Jake was instantly struck by the smell of pine wafting in the air. His sister used the same cleaning product their mother had, and it brought him back to a happier, less complicated time. To be there, if only for a moment, comforted him.

While his niece pulled him down the hallway, her tiny hand squeezing his, Silla stepped out of the kitchen archway. Her lips instantly turned up into a smile when she saw him. "Why didn't you call to tell me you were stopping by?"

"It's much more fun to surprise you."

She smacked him on the arm and pulled him in for a hug. "You are staying for supper, right?"

"I'd like that. Gabe wants me to beat him on a video game afterward." Jake winked at his nephew.

The boy snorted. "You wish."

"Okay, if you want to do that," Silla said to her children. "Go on upstairs to your rooms and do your homework. I want to talk to your uncle alone right now."

Without hesitation, they scrambled up the staircase.

"You have them trained." Jake followed his sister into the kitchen.

"I was taught by the best."

"True. Mom always could crack that imaginary whip."

"So, why the impromptu visit?" Her hazel eyes focused on his.

Jake took a seat on a barstool next to the large, granite-top island that separated the kitchen from the dining area and shrugged. "What? I can't come by to see my niece and nephews?"

His sister frowned, then turned to open the refrigerator, pulled out a bottle of beer, and handed it to him. "Tell me what's going on."

Silla knew him too well. That might be a problem.

"I have to go away for a story. I might be gone for a month or so."

She studied him for what seemed like an eternity, causing sweat to bead down between his shoulder blades. "Have you told Mom?"

Jake swallowed hard. Damn it all to hell. She knew something was up. "No. I thought you could tell her."

"Why me? What are you afraid of?"

"Nothing." He shifted on the stool. "This came up suddenly, and I wanted to see the kids before I go. Anything wrong with that?"

Her intense eyes narrowed as she tucked a strand of her dark, curly hair behind her ear. "Not at all as long as you're telling the truth."

"Why would I be lying?"

"I don't know, Jake, but there's a reason why you're afraid to tell Mom you're going somewhere."

"Pfftt, I'm not afraid, Silla. Why would you think that?"

"Because Mom would, and you assume I'm not smart enough to see through your bullshit like she can."

Crap. This exchange wasn't supposed to go down this way. How was he going to get out of this without spilling his guts about what he was truly doing? He loved Silla too much to cause her to worry, and he knew if he told her what he was about to do, she most certainly would.

****

Meghan Gentry wanted to scream bloody murder but held her tongue instead and smiled her most polite smile. "No, I'm sorry, I can't."

"Why not?" Felix Rim stood at the drugstore counter staring hard at her, his brown eyes growing darker, more sinister by the second.

This was the tenth time the guy had asked her out, and the tenth time she'd said no. The first couple, she found somewhat endearing. After the sixth, she was downright annoyed. Now, he scared her. Some men didn't like to be rejected. This one was becoming belligerent about it.

Even if she had time to date, which she didn't, it wouldn't be with Felix. Not after learning of his affiliation with a local supremacist group. Meghan did not want anything to do with that kind of hate. She'd had enough of that growing up.

"Is everything okay, Meghan?" Pharmacist Lyle Strom asked, his seventy-five-year-old weathered face wrinkling more than usual. His concern for her was palpable, and he'd voiced that worry on numerous occasions. Meghan was new to Brooksville, Missouri. Lyle had lived there all his life. He knew everyone in town and the Rims, according to him, were bad to the bone.

"Mr. Rim was just leaving. Right, Felix?"

The man sneered at her boss, and deliberately slammed against a rack, knocking some pregnancy test boxes off the shelf as he made his way toward the door.

Meghan closed her eyes and took in a cleansing breath. "I'll go pick those up."

"I have half a mind to ban him from the store." Lyle pointed an arthritic finger toward the exit.

She walked around the counter and placed the kits one by one back on the shelf. "You don't need that kind of trouble, Lyle. I can deal with Felix."

"That numb-nuts can't seem to understand that you're not interested. That worries me. Felix Rim harassed another gal at the local café about three years back. The girl up and left town because of it. I don't want that to happen to you. You're the best worker I've ever had."

Meghan smiled. Lyle was like a grandfather to her, and his admiration made her love him even more. "I can handle him. Don't worry about me."

"I can't help but be concerned since you live so far out of town in that ram-shackled house with barely a door latch for security."

"Nonsense. It takes me ten minutes to get here. That means it'd take Deputy Stockman seven minutes to get to me."

The older man snorted. "I'd say six with that heavy foot. But still, you could get killed in six minutes, Meghan. Maybe getting a dog would help."

She shook her head. "I work too many hours to have a pet. It would be left alone all the time. I couldn't do that to an animal.

"How about a gun?"

Meghan's jaw dropped. She'd never owned one. More gun owners were shot doing stupid things. She'd be one of them. *No thank you.*

"I'll be fine, Lyle. You're going to worry yourself sick. That heart of yours can't handle it."

"My ticker's just fine, missy. Don't you go worrying your blonde head about me."

She reached across the counter and squeezed his arm. "Okay, if you promise to do the same. I'm a big girl. I can take care of myself."

"Big," he said, his hazel eyes looking her up and down. "What are you? A hundred pounds wet?"

The jingle of the front door saved her from

answering. The reprieve was cut short when she saw that it was Mrs. Ferguson. The woman was a hypochondriac and came in every other day with a new complaint.

She spotted Meghan and strode toward her, her grayish eyes looking bloodshot, her pallor almost orange. Something wasn't right with the woman.

"Meghan, I need your help."

"What can I do for you?"

The woman huffed at the question. "You can't guess?"

Meghan shrugged. "What?"

"My God. It's my skin, girl. I look like a carrot."

"Is it something you ingested, or a self-tanner?" Meghan had no clue what she was supposed to do.

"Seriously? Why would a woman my age care about having a glow? Besides, this would never be a desired color for anyone, would it?"

"So, you're saying it's something you're taking that caused the color change?"

"Yes. What could it be?"

Meghan had no idea and looked to Lyle for help.

He stared at the woman's face, rubbing at his square, stubbled chin, looking perplexed.

"Well," Mrs. Ferguson prompted. "What is wrong with me?"

"Either your liver is failing, or you've been taking in too much Beta Carotene. Which is it?" Lyle asked.

"How much is too much?" the older woman asked.

"If you have to ask, it's probably too much. Stop taking it and see if your normal color returns. If it doesn't, go get some bloodwork done." Lyle had had enough of the woman as well.

"That's it? You don't have some pill I can take?"

"Are you serious, woman? A pill got you here in the first place, so no, I don't. But you know what might help?" Lyle gave Meghan a cockeyed grin and looked back at the lady in question.

Mrs. Ferguson's eyes lit up with excitement. "What?

"A shrink."

"Well, I never," she huffed. "See if I ever come back here."

"That's your prerogative."

Meghan inwardly applauded her boss. It'd been a nightmare dealing with this woman for the past year. If Lyle's condemnation kept her from coming in, she was all for it. Mrs. Ferguson needed a therapist, not another drug, and maybe his bluntness would finally make her see that. If nothing else, she'd be someone else's problem, not theirs.

Chapter Two

"You'll be pulling your weight while you're here, Jackson." Bobby Rudow led Jake to a back room where a twin-sized bed and a badly dinged-up, three-drawer dresser filled the space. This was going to be his home for the next few months. Thank God he wasn't claustrophobic. Otherwise, life would be pure hell.

"I'll let you get settled in and put your things away. When Andrew's free, I'll come to get you. Since he runs things around here, he'll want to go over what he expects from you."

"Okay. Thanks." Jake took a seat on the bed, the box springs groaning under his weight.

Once Bobby had gone, he blew out a breath, questioning the sanity of this plan. The people he'd met were nothing like he was used to. The men in the compound had shaved heads, tattoos from here to there, some bizarre beyond words. He'd seen pictures of supremacists before, but that's as far as it'd gone. This was the real deal, and it gave him a sense of dread.

When he'd first met Bobby at the warehouse, he was frisked, his bag checked, and questioned for three hours about his background, all fabricated for his safety by a friend of his. Jackson Gallagher didn't exist. It was a made-up persona; one he'd introduced himself as in numerous chatrooms to get to know the right people over some time.

Now, here he was. Inside. About to be indoctrinated into a group that he never wanted any part of until he was rumored to be one because of a story someone had led him to—a byline that now he had time to think about it, was a plant, to sink his career in journalism, and make him unhireable to any other reputable news affiliation. By someone he thought of as a friend. The man who now had his job at NewsCo.

Some friend. If it took him a lifetime, he'd find a way to get even.

Jake reached down onto the floor for his bag and opened the zipper, removing the clothes he'd brought, all old jeans and T-shirts so he'd fit in. Hopefully, he'd have free time to go into town and get some writing material so he could keep notes on what he learned while he was there, though he'd have to hide them. Trust was earned here according to Bobby, and he was starting from the bottom of the trust chain.

After Jake had put his clothes in the dresser, he paced the floor, anxious and apprehensive about meeting Andrew Gibson. He was the so-called leader of the BWN and wielded a lot of power in Brooksville. To say he was nervous to face him would have been an understatement. What if the guy saw through his ruse? Could he get out of the compound with his head intact? Just the thought had the hairs on the back of his neck standing on end.

This whole thing was crazy. He should get out now before it was too late.

A knock drew him to the door where Bobby stood. "Andrew's ready to see you."

Jake followed him down the hallway from where they'd come earlier and turned right through a set of archways, another long hall, and into a door where a redheaded man with freckled skin sat lounging behind a cluttered desk. The room was much larger in comparison to his bedroom, yet felt smaller, almost stifling in the man's presence.

He pointed to one of the two chairs in front of him. "Take a seat, Jackson."

Jake did as he was told, all the while studying him. He wasn't a large guy by any means, but he held a hint of danger that kept Jake on edge. Maybe because of what he represented and what little Bobby had told him about Gibson's activities.

"So, you want to be a part of our organization?"

"I do," Jake lied.

"You're going to have to earn your wings here. I'll expect a lot from you before anything is given. Do you understand that?"

"Yes. I understand."

"We have some rules that need to be followed. If you break one, you're out."

"All right. Do you have a list of these rules?"

"Bobby will fill you in on them. But the most important one for you to always remember is that I expect loyalty above everything else. You give me that and all will go smoothly."

Jake swallowed hard. What was he supposed to say? He wasn't sure what Gibson wanted to hear. "I can do that."

"Good. Glad to hear it. It's getting close to dinnertime. Bobby will take you to the kitchen. I want you to help prepare the meal tonight. Any problem with that?"

"Not at all." Jake stood and turned to Bobby. "I'll follow you."

"I like that go-gett'm attitude." Andrew rose from his seat, exposing the Nazi symbol on his belt buckle. "I think this is going to work out well. I'll see you at dinner."

Jake fought not to scowl. People who wore insignias like that made him sick. He shook it off as he was led to the back of the compound where the kitchen was located. Six women were there, three wearing tank tops and cut-off shorts, one very pregnant, all talking with each other until they spotted him. All but one stared daggers at him, the other doing an up and down with her eyes like he was a rack of lamb.

"Jackson's here to help you ladies. Give him a job and he'll do it," Bobby said, grinning like a Cheshire cat. He found it amusing that Jake was the only man to help with meal preparation.

Whatever. Jake knew how to cook. That was one thing his mother had insisted he learn growing up.

"What do you need me to do?" he asked the women, ready for anything they threw his way.

"Can you peel potatoes?" a petite brunette asked, looking annoyed that he was there.

"I can." He rubbed his hands together.

Every one of them appeared surprised.

One tossed him a paring knife and pointed to the bags of potatoes.

Jake went right to work, glancing up now and then to see the group busying themselves while watching his progress. To him, they weren't used to seeing a man doing domestic chores. *Boy*, were they going to be surprised by his abilities. He'd worked his share of holidays at homeless shelters, another thing his mother had insisted on. So, he knew how to feed a large group of people. That was a piece of cake. Getting these women to trust him was going to be the difficult part, yet to get his story, he needed to do that, or die trying.

****

Meghan stepped out of the back room carrying a large box right as she heard the front door jiggling. When she reached the counter and placed the cardboard container on the floor, a tall, dark-headed man started down the paper aisle. She'd never seen him before, and since being a resident for over a year, she knew almost everyone in town.

"Can I help you find something?" she asked, suddenly intrigued by the stranger.

He turned toward her, and she sucked in a deep breath. His eyes were almost eerie, a crystal blue that contrasted amazingly with his mop of dark, wavy hair. He was handsome beyond words, and she found herself staring, angry with herself when her mouth inched open.

"I'm looking for writing material. I think I can find what I need, though. Thanks." He went back to looking at the shelf filled with notebooks, calendars, and writing supplies.

He didn't need her help. Maybe he was just annoyed with women's attention. Looks like his surely got a lot of it and he could have anyone. Meghan wasn't a super model. Probably too plain for the likes of him. The thought made her snort—an unladylike sound that he heard and turned back to acknowledge.

"Is there a problem?" He grabbed a couple of plain notebooks, a packet of pens and walked toward her. The man moved like a jungle cat, with a swagger like no one she'd ever seen. He wore a simple, white, V-neck tee that stretched taut across a muscular chest and nicely formed biceps. His jeans were old and weathered but fit his narrow hips snugly, not that unflattering baggy look that the young guys seemed to find in vogue.

Meghan shook her head, trying hard to calm her racing pulse.

"I'll take these," he said, placing the supplies down on the counter and extracting his wallet.

With shaky hands, she reached for each item, running it over the scanner and bagged them up. "Fifteen, fifty-eight please."

He pulled out a twenty, his finger brushing against hers as he thrust it her way, causing an electric current to shoot up her arm.

She quickly gave him his change, wondering if he'd had the same reaction. Seemed that he didn't by his demeaner. *Figures.* The only time she had a strange feeling for someone, and he didn't give her a second look.

Oh, well. She didn't date anyway, and she'd never be all gaga for a man who had no interest in her. That would make her as bad as Felix and she never wanted to stoop to such a level—not ever.

"Have a nice day." She reached for the box she'd brought from the storage room. She needed to price everything inside and get them shelved before closing for the day.

When the jiggling door signaled that he'd gone, Meghan blew out a breath. Hopefully, he wouldn't be back. She'd never seen him before, so he was passing through and that was for the best.

An hour later, Meghan set the alarm and locked the back door. Lyle had gone to the bank to deposit the weekly earnings, an event that happened every Friday afternoon.

She reached into her purse for her keys and was headed for her car when Felix came around the side of the building.

Her heart took off on an uphill spiral. Could she get to the door and lock it before he got to her? If she did, maybe it'd just piss him off more.

"I don't have time to talk, Felix. I have to get home," she said, hoping her words would deter him.

They didn't. He just smiled a creepy smile, revealing a mouth of crooked teeth. His hair looked like it hadn't been washed in a week. Everything about him gave her the willies.

"This won't take long." He caught her as she opened the car door and grasped her arm to keep her from getting inside.

"Let go of me."

"Why? What you gonna do? I don't see Lyle skulking around to save you right now. Not that the old fart could do anything. He should have retired ten years ago."

Meghan might have been afraid of Felix Rim, but her protective nature for the old man he was cutting down kicked in before her common sense could. "Lyle Strom is the kindest man I've ever known. So, you can just take your angry words and fuck off."

"Whoa, the mouth on that girl. Maybe I should wash it out with my cum." He squeezed his crotch for emphasis.

Now Meghan was worried. This man had never been disgusting in his pursuit. This was a new low for him, and it terrified her.

"Leave me alone," she said, yanking her arm from

his grasp.

Immediately, he grabbed a handful of her hair and dragged her down to her knees so that she was positioned in front of his cock and started to unzip his pants.

She screamed and tried to get loose.

"Something going on here?" someone asked.

Meghan turned her head, pain shooting through her scalp, and saw the stranger from before.

"This is none of your business. Move on." Felix cussed under his breath when the man started toward them.

"I'm thinking the lady isn't in agreement on this." The stranger's eyes narrowed like daggers on Felix. He was twice his size and towered over him now.

Felix's grip slackened and Meghan took the opportunity to pull away and stumble to her feet.

"That your car?" He pointed to her vehicle.

"Yes," she said, her voice trembling.

"You might want to get inside and go. I'll stay and take care of this."

She nodded, jumped in her car and started the engine. Without looking back, she took off, her hands barely able to control the wheel because they were shaking so much.

She wasn't worried about the stranger. He could take Felix in a heartbeat. No, Meghan was apprehensive about running into Rim again. If he'd gone this far today in public, what would happen the next time they met somewhere more secluded? What were the odds that her Knight in Shining Armor would come along again and save her? Probably slim to none, and that didn't bode well for her—not one bit. Somehow, she'd need to protect herself.

Perhaps Lyle was right. Maybe she did need that gun he spoke of, and she'd have to learn how to use it without shooting off her foot.

Chapter Three

Jake stood with his fist clenched tight, glaring at the man beside him. Seeing the scumbag again made him want to punch his lights out. What was he doing at the compound?

"Felix, here, says you got in his face yesterday. Is that true?" Andrew asked in a calm, yet stern voice as he sat at his desk.

"Yeah, I did. Why? Who is he to you?"

"He's one of my right-hand men, Jackson. Care to explain yourself before I send you packing?"

What were the odds? "He was forcing himself on a young lady behind the pharmacy. I stopped him."

Andrew's eyes narrowed. "Is this true, Rim?"

Felix scowled and his eyes filled with scorn. "It's that fucking bitch, Meghan. You know I've been after that piece of ass for six months now. She's nothing but a cock tease."

"We don't need this kind of trouble. Sheriff Hanson is already watching us closely because of the Kennett disappearance. Leave the girl alone. Understand? We have plenty of willing ladies here you can screw to your heart's content."

"But—"

Andrew slammed his hand on top of the desk, sending a pile of papers fluttering to the floor. "You listen, and you listen good. Leave Meghan alone. I hear anything about you even going near the Strom Pharmacy and I'll string you up by the balls."

The man's face paled. "Okay, boss. Whatever you say."

Jake clenched his teeth, trying to grasp what he'd heard while controlling his anger. Gibson either had a line in the sand, or he was protecting himself from something that occurred before Jake got there. Something about some guy named Kennett. Was there a story behind that name? Could he uncover what it was without revealing his identity? That was the million-dollar question. Was it worth it for him to find the answers?

"You can go, Felix. I want to talk to Jackson."

Rim scowled again at Jake and left the room.

Great, now he had an enemy here—one he didn't need.

"Loyalty for all the men here is important to me, Jackson. I get that you didn't know Felix. Spend a few days meeting everyone so you'll know next time."

Jake's jaw slacked. "So, you're saying I should have let him force himself on her because he's one of us? If that's the case, I'm not sure I want to be a part of this brotherhood." He was taking a chance at getting kicked out, but he needed to know how far Gibson's standards went. Rape wasn't something he could abide, not even to save his career in journalism. If it was acceptable in this compound, Jake was leaving.

"No, Jackson. That's not what I'm saying. You heard me tell Felix to back off. I'd like you to stay. I assure you I don't condone that kind of shit."

"Glad to hear it. You might want to tell Felix that. He doesn't think it's wrong."

"I'll talk to him. Now, you can go. I've got to get to a meeting and I'm already late."

Jake nodded.

After he left his office, Jake's mind spun a mile a minute. He'd need to do some research on this Kennett character. Find out when he went missing and the particulars around the event. He now had a lead to follow and he planned to do that.

He strode down the hall and turned the corner, practically colliding with one of the gals from the kitchen—the one who'd ogled him the day before.

"I was hoping to run into you," she said, batting a pair of false eyelashes.

Oh, shit. Just what I need. A White Supremacist vying for my affection.

"Yeah? Why were you looking for me?" He thought he could use her interest to his advantage. Maybe he could learn something from her.

"I needed a big, strong man to lift something heavy."

"Sure. What do you need me to move?"

"Some food crates came in and I need you to carry them to the pantry."

"I can do that. Lead the way."

They both headed for the kitchen. Inside the huge room, Jake saw six large crates on the floor—containers that didn't look like they'd have food in them. They looked more like gun crates.

"Where do you get your food?" he asked as casually as he could. Jake didn't want her to be suspicious of the question.

"One of the local grocers supplies us once a month. Friends of the cause."

He walked over to the crates. "Where's the pantry?"

She pointed to the door across from the huge, industrial-like refrigerator. Where did they get such a thing and how much did it cost? Now that he thought about it, the six-burner stove and dishwasher were all state of the art. Something was fishy here and it wasn't coming from those crates.

Brushing off the thought, Jake went to open the pantry door, then returned to the boxes, hefting one up into his arms and lugging it to the room. He stacked them two by two on the ground and walked back into the kitchen and closed the door. "Anything else you need me to do?"

The woman sighed. "No. Not right now but in a few hours, you can come back and help prepare dinner. We may have to run to town for a few other things also. You have a large vehicle, right?"

"I do. I'll see you in a few hours."

Jake left the room. Somehow, he was going to get into that pantry and look inside those crates. Either they were filled with heavy canned goods or guns. He needed to know which.

If indeed they were weapons, why would Andrew need so many? What was he planning? If it was something Jake could prevent, he was going to do so. Lives could be at stake.

Back in his room, he reached under the dresser for his notebook and pen and wrote some of the things he'd learned that day. He jotted down about the crates and this Kennett man. Andrew meeting with someone. Who could that have been, and did it have anything to do with what was inside those boxes?

Shit. Some way, he had to see what was in them. *Tonight*. After everyone went to bed. He'd have to pray he didn't get caught, or he'd end up like this Kennett character—missing in action.

****

Meghan stared at the display case in Black Powder Firearms, almost sick at the idea of buying a gun. It was stupid yet necessary since her run-in with Rim.

"See anything you like?" Charlie Hall, the barrel-chested owner asked.

"What do you suggest?"

"For you, something light and easy to handle. I have this small Smith & Wesson." He slid the glass case door open and removed a handgun and held it out to her.

She swallowed hard. With a shaky hand, she took the weapon and clasped it tight. What was she doing? Owning a gun was the last thing she wanted to do. The twinge from her scalp helped remind her of why she needed one. Meghan was so conflicted. She didn't know what to do.

"That little beauty will set you back seven-hundred and eighty-six dollars."

Meghan's jaw dropped. No way could she afford that. She was living paycheck to paycheck now. She wouldn't eat for six months if she bought the gun.

She handed it back and shook her head. "Sorry. Can't afford that. Thanks for your time, though, Charlie."

"No problem. If you change your mind, it'll be here."

She smiled at the older man and turned to leave.

As she stepped out the door, she saw Andrew Gibson getting out of his pickup. Meghan knew he ran the compound east of town—the same Klan that Rim was a part of. Apparently, those people had no respect for the rule of law.

She held her head high and started for her car.

"Morning, Miss Gentry. I wanted to tell you I had a talk with Felix about his actions yesterday with you. You need not worry about it ever happening again."

What did he mean by that? Had Felix confessed his attack? "Who told you about yesterday?"

"Jackson Gallagher. I'm truly sorry for Rim's actions."

She shook her head. "Who's Jackson Gallagher?"

"He's one of our new members. He said he stopped Felix from hurting you, and like I said, it'll never happen again. I've told Felix to stay away from you."

The stranger was one of them? Meghan never would have thought he'd be a supremacist. That meant he'd be staying in Brooksville. Which had no bearing now since the man was a blemish in her eyes—the kiss of death in her book and she'd never want anything to do with him.

"Thanks." She stepped away and walked to her car.

Andrew Gibson was trouble and so was anyone who was affiliated with the man, and that meant the gorgeous stranger.

Once she was behind the wheel, she realized one thing. If nothing else, she'd never have to deal with Felix again. He wouldn't cross his boss in any way. That made her more at ease. Now, she could continue to live her life like she had since she'd moved to Brooksville. Everything could go back to normal.

On her way home, she stopped at the grocery store. She'd pick up a few things since she didn't have to buy a gun.

The store was almost empty as she moved down the aisle, grabbing a tin of coffee and some green tea. As she turned the corner, her breath caught in her chest. *He was here. That Jackson guy.* With two women she recognized from the compound who came into the pharmacy to pick up their birth control pills. They had two shopping carts full of food and were headed for the cashier's counter. If Andrew's words weren't enough, here was proof that the man was a part of that despicable group. How could anyone hate so much that they'd be a part of something so dark and menacing? Meghan would never understand it.

She turned down the next aisle, determined to get her shopping done and prayed they'd be gone by the time she was finished. On the turnaround, her luck ended, and she came face-to-face with the man himself. He carried a case of beer in his hand, his crystal blue eyes widening when he saw her. "Hello." He smiled, revealing stunningly white teeth.

Meghan didn't return the gesture. She didn't even want to respond. Yes, he'd helped her when she needed him to, but he could be as dangerous as Rim.

"I gotta go." She maneuvered her cart around him and took off. It was rude, true, but hopefully, he'd realized she didn't want any part of him.

Meghan rushed down the last aisle and used the self-checkout, afraid to look to see if he was still there. She needed to get out of the store and go home. This Jackson Gallagher was not her friend. He was nobody to her, and he would remain so from this day forward.

Chapter Four

Jake lay atop the lumpy mattress and released a weary breath. It was going to be a long night. He'd have to wait hours before he snuck into the kitchen pantry to see what was in those crates, something that could get him in big trouble if he got caught. But he refused to let that stop him.

If guns were inside, he'd need to find out what Gibson planned to do with them so that no one got hurt. There had been too much senseless gun violence in the past. He didn't want any more in the future. Not if he could prevent it somehow.

He raised his head and folded the cheap, under-filled pillow, trying to get comfortable. He still wondered about Meghan's reaction in the grocery store earlier today. She completely blew him off, kind of like he had when he'd first met her. Maybe that's why she'd done it—to get even. Not that it mattered. Jake wasn't here to socialize with the town's people anyway, but he'd helped her, and for whatever reason, her rebuff had stung.

He had to admit that she was a pretty little thing, and if he had to wager a bet, she weighed less than his sister who was rail thin. Both fragile and vulnerable. That alone brought out the protectiveness in him.

Her hair was light blonde and shiny, with coppery highlights, her large eyes as green as a sparkling, multi-faceted emerald. He'd think about dating her under different circumstances. Yet, he wasn't there to find a girlfriend. He was there to save his tainted career.

The thought brought him back to his plan. That even proved futile at learning anything from the women while fixing dinner. Everyone seemed tight-lipped about discussing anything. Were they like this with everyone or just him—the new guy. Maybe he had to earn their trust, like Andrew had said when they'd first met.

Hopefully, in a few more days, they would slip up and start talking. Perhaps Jake would catch something useful. He did manage to get names tonight. Amber was the gal who had an interest in him. He was going to use that, even though the thought troubled him. Jake hadn't deliberately hurt any woman. His parents had taught him better than that. But, in this case, he might have to, especially if doing so could save lives.

Jake's eyes grew heavy, and as he started to nod off, he heard a loud pop and sat up in bed. What was that? Was it a car backfiring outside, or a gunshot?

He rose and slipped out the door and moved down the hall toward the front of the compound. Another pop had him flattening himself against the wall. It sounded like it had come from inside the building.

Voices from close by made Jake hold his breath. When he thought it was safe to move, he started down the hall again, trying to figure out which direction the sound had come from. He hadn't been to the east side of the compound. Maybe they had some sort of firing range there, though it was awful late in the evening for target practice.

As he reached the large gathering area, another *pop, pop, pop* signaled to Jake that he was traveling in the right direction. He moved through another long hall, inching his way slowly in case someone came out of a door. The last thing he wanted was to get caught.

At the end of the hall, there was a light illuminating an archway twenty or so feet ahead, which meant someone was probably inside. Should he hedge his bets and get closer, or should he stay put and wait, hoping to hear something?

Jake didn't know what to do.

He choice was taken from him when Felix and another man he didn't recognize came into view and headed his way.

Jake backtracked to the large front room and hid behind a curtain.

The two men stopped a few feet from him, and his heart started to hammer. Had they seen him? All he needed was for Felix to have something over his head.

"Don't tell Andrew about that shipment," Felix said. "What he doesn't know won't hurt him."

"Yes, but if he learns about it, he might just kill you," the other man said.

"I'm not worried about Gibson. He's too busy with other endeavors to notice a few crates of guns. Right now, he's off trying to secure a source from a local farmer."

"I still think you should hide them somewhere. Especially if he's doing what you're saying. If he gets a new food source, he'll need to put it in the pantry where the guns are."

"You might be right. I'll find a place for them—somewhere he'd never look. Now, though, I'm going to find myself a warm pussy. You do the same."

Once they were gone, Jake released the breath he'd been holding. *Christ.* This Rim character had no loyalty or morality. Not the right-hand man that Gibson thought he was for sure. But was that any skin off Jake's back? Not really. Why should he care about any of these people? They were all neo-fascist creeps and deserved whatever they got. At least he knew now that those were indeed guns in the crates, though Rim being behind the purchase only worried him more. Not since the guy had no qualms about forcing himself on a woman. Shooting someone was probably second nature to him.

Jake came from behind the curtain and started down the hall to his room. He needed to write all this down, and he'd get some sleep. In the morning, he'd think about Rim and figure out what he was going to do about the man.

****

Meghan and her best friend, Lily Parsons stepped into Baby Makes Three, intent on looking for a shower gift.

"So, we know Vi is having a girl. How about we go halves on one of her registry items?" Lily asked, glancing around the store.

Meghan nodded. "Sounds perfect. Let's see what's on her list and go from there."

The two walked up to the shop owner who was standing behind the cashier's glass counter.

"Can we get a copy of Violet's list?" Meghan asked, smiling at the woman.

"You are the third one today." She reached under the counter and pulled out a slip of paper and handed it to her.

"Has any of these items been bought?" Lily pointed to the list in Meghan's hand.

"Yes. Let me cross them off for you."

Meghan handed the list back and took it again when she'd completed the task. The two went to look around.

"What do you think?" Meghan looked at her best friend. "The baby swing or the rocking chair?"

"If we get the swing, we can also get a few cute outfits and a box of those fancy diapers she wanted."

Meghan agreed. "Let's go with the swing, and I'm going to let you wrap it all up with your creative flare. You know I'm not good at that."

"I think you underestimate yourself, but I'll take care of the presentation."

Meghan walked to a rack of newborn outfits, half the row for boys, the other half girls. Everything was adorable, and it took her and Lily a while to choose three, thicker infant sleepers and hats to match.

The weather had started to cool now that Summer was officially over, all her girlfriends blabbing away about this coming Halloween. Meghan didn't get all crazy about the holiday—wasn't into the scary costumes and horror movies that aired every hour on the hour. It just wasn't her thing, especially with her upbringing.

She was never allowed to go trick or treating growing up, her father saying it was a Pagan ritual and went against his religious beliefs. Everything did. Christmas was all about celebrating the birth of Christ, not opening presents, not that they could afford them anyway. No. All the money her mother earned working at the school cafeteria went for bottles of whiskey that her father sanctioned since Jesus enjoyed his wine. Boy could that man cherry-pick his Bible verses.

"You okay?" Lily placed a hand on her arm.

Meghan nodded, angry that she let such a troubling memory resurface at such a happy time. She was excited for her friend. A new baby brought new beginnings and Meghan was all about starting over. That's why she was here in Brooksville.

"After we get everything into the trunk of my car, let's go to Culvert's and get an ice cream. I'm craving the strawberry cheesecake flavor."

"Sure, I was wanting to try their new mocha and cake batter shake that Lyle said was so tasty."

Lily grinned. "Of course, he did. Oh, I have to tell you about this guy I saw a couple days ago. I was driving by during my lunch hour, and he was walking down Main Street. I'd never seen him in town before but man oh man he was gorgeous. He had this head of wavy, raven hair and stunning, light-colored eyes, and he was built like a model."

"Stop, I know who he is. You don't want anything to do with him."

Her friend frowned. "Why? Who is he?"

"Jackson something or other and he's part of Gibson's crew."

"What? Well, that's disappointing."

Meghan agreed. It was disillusioning to say the least. No one should be involved with that type of hate group. Any kind of cult-like atmosphere was troubling, including a religious affiliation that promoted exclusion like her dad's church had. That, and her father himself, had drove her away from Christ church and would keep her from ever going back. She just couldn't take that atmosphere again.

Meghan shook her head. What was the reason her mind kept meandering back to that life? Those troubling memories needed to stay where they belonged—in the past.

"Come on," she said, grabbing the large bag and handing her friend the other. "Let's get that ice cream. It's so much better than any man could ever be."

Lily snorted. "You just haven't been with the right one. But we can talk about that at Culvert's."

On the way down Main Street, Meghan pushed all the negative thoughts away. Her life was good now, especially since she no longer had to worry about Felix.

Lily pulled her car into the parlor's parking lot, and the two made their way inside. There was a line of people waiting to order and Meghan glanced around, her gaze landing on those eerie, crystal blue eyes for a third time in a week. Jackson sat with Andrew Gibson and Cullen Hatfield, the two men who ran the BWN compound. Gibson was the brains of the outfit, Hatfield, the muscle, and rumor had it that they made a local businessman disappear—an event that happened just weeks prior to her moving to town.

Meghan looked away, unnerved by him being there. Why the reaction? She knew he was bad news, yet for some reason her body didn't care about that. It caused a strange, tingling feeling to cascade across her skin.

"Let's get our ice cream and go outside," she said to Lily.

Lily had spotted Jackson as well and was staring at him like he was the ice cream she was about to order. God, what was his appeal? Was it those eyes? They were unique. Yet, you might as well say the man was a Nazi. No normal person would be attracted to that. Would they?

Meghan glanced at him again. Okay, maybe they could, but there was no future in it. Look at what had happened to her mother, a hard-working woman who fell for a fanatic, now just a shell of a woman. Any form of zealotry was destructive, and Meghan refused to let that happen to her like her mom had. She'd grown much too wise for that life filled with misery.

Chapter Five

Jake saw her and he couldn't look away. What was it about the woman that seemed to divert his attention from his goal of getting a story?

He swallowed a hard lump in his throat and turned away.

"What do you think of that, Gallagher?"

"Huh." He looked from one man to the other.

"She's a pretty girl but Rim would go ballistic if he found out you liked her," Gibson said, his attention also on Meghan.

"The brunette she's with, Lily Parsons, is single. She's also not off limits."

Jake studied the woman a moment. She was every bit as pretty as Meghan, but he didn't find himself drawn to her like the blonde.

"I heard Amber has the hots for you," Cullen said matter of factly. "She might be a better option."

Nope. Not going to happen. No way was Jake dating anyone from the compound. They all promoted hate and divisiveness—something he couldn't abide.

"I'll think about it," he lied and took a sip of his coffee. He still wasn't sure why he was invited to join the two men on their trip to town. So far, all they'd done was sit in Culvert's.

This was the first time he'd met Hatfield, a big, brawny guy with a bald head and a snake tattoo crawling through a skull on his arm. The man was intimidating to say the least. Jake wouldn't want an altercation with him.

"Care to tell me why I'm here?"

"Does there have to be a reason? I just thought it'd be a chance for you to get to know Cullen and I better, and for us to do the same."

"All right. What do you want to know?" Jake asked. This was an opportunity to use the profile he'd created for Jackson Gallagher, something he'd worked for weeks on to assimilate with BWN. A troubled upbringing in a foster care environment, not easily checked and fueled by poor, white resentment. A perfect place for fostering hate. So unlike his real-life experience.

"Where did you grow up?" Cullen asked, taking a gulp of his soda.

"Do we have all day?"

Both men squinted their eyes.

"I spent time in about twelve different foster homes. Some not so bad. A few not healthy environments for a young mind to be molded."

"Sorry to hear that," Andrew said, not at all looking sad about his story. Jake assumed it was empty words from a man who could care less.

"No need to be. I learned fast to only rely on myself."

"Lemons into lemonade type of thing, right?" Cullen said, glancing out the window and nodding to Andrew.

"We'll be right back." Gibson rose from the booth seat. "Stay here and hold our table. We have someone we need to speak with." Both left the building, walking past the same window and down the sidewalk toward a man in a suit who was three car lengths ahead of them. Who was he and what did Andrew and Cullen want with him. *To be a fly on the wall of that conversation.* Jake would just wait and hope he'd learn. He took another sip of his coffee and turned his attention to the line in front of the counter.

Why was Meghan so different with him since his visit to the pharmacy?

Wait. Maybe she knew he lived in the compound now. A lot of people hated White Supremacy. He was one of them. But she didn't know he was undercover for a story. She thought he was one of them. True enough, that could very well be her reason for the brush off and he couldn't blame her. On the flipside, he'd do the same.

She and her friend got their ice cream and left the shop, not bothering to look his way again.

It was for the best anyway. He needed to focus on his story, not some pretty blonde who thought the worst of him and could blow away in a gale force wind.

Jake couldn't help but smile at the image. He returned his attention to the window and was struck dumb by Meghan who now sat at a table topped with a red and white striped umbrella. Her face was flushed from laughing and he was mesmerized. The woman was nothing like any of the women he'd dated in the past, which was bizarre in itself. Brunettes like her friend had been more his preference, but there was just something about her that he found intriguing.

Past Meghan, Jake saw Andrew, Cullen, and the man they'd been following at a Range Rover just beyond the outside sitting area. The man looked annoyed at the two, his body language tense. Jake wished he could read lips since the three were arguing about something. If he had a phone, he'd get a shot of the guy and his plate and have a friend who worked at the DMV check the registration. Unfortunately, he was going to have to do everything the hard way—all on his own.

The man gave Andrew a gesture that could only be construed as fuck off and got in the SUV and pulled away from the curb. What the hell was that all about. He'd give his left testicle to know, though if Andrew got wind of what Jake was doing, he'd probably lose more than that.

****

Meghan climbed into bed and turned off the light, so tired she could barely keep her eyes open. As she was drifting off to sleep, a car door slamming had her sitting up straight, her heart hammering in her chest.

She shoved the covers aside and raced to the window, looking out to see where the vehicle was parked. She didn't have close neighbors. Whoever was here was not expected.

A movement caught her eye, and she trained in on the area, noting a shadowy outline cast next to a few cedar trees against the fence line. Her first thought was Felix had gone against Andrew's wishes and had come to harm her.

She sprinted back to the bed and grabbed her phone off the side table and dialed 9-1-1. Her hands trembled as she snuck down the hall to the front door, making sure the bolt lock was in place.

"9-1-1 dispatch. What is your emergency?"

"Someone is outside my house lurking around." Meghan crept to the back to check the chain on the rear exit. It was secure.

"Okay. We'll send a deputy out to check. Stay on the line until he gets there. Did you get a look at this person? Is it a man or woman?"

"No, I didn't, and I'm not sure."

"That's okay. Try not to worry. The officer's on his way. How were you alerted to this prowler?" the female dispatcher asked in a calm tone.

"I was about to go to sleep and heard a car door close. I looked out and saw a figure in the distance."

"Are all the doors locked?"

"Yes. I just checked."

"The deputy is six minutes out. Hang on."

"Okay," she said, her voice shaky.

"Do you have an ex-husband or boyfriend that it could be?"

"No. I've never been married, and I haven't dated anyone since I moved to Brooksville over a year ago."

"Maybe one you left your last town for?" she suggested.

No way. Tom Harken would never come looking for her. The man was too busy admiring himself in a mirror to care about anyone else.

"No chance of that, sorry," Meghan told her. "I do have someone who has been bothering me lately. It might be him."

"Do you have a name?"

"Felix Rim. He's been nasty since I told him I didn't want to go out with him."

"I've contacted the officer and he's a few minutes out. Can you tell me what he's done to make you think it could be him?"

"He cornered me after work. It wasn't a pleasant encounter."

"Can you still see this person outside?" the dispatcher asked.

Meghan glanced out the window. The shadowy image was still outlined next to the trees.

"Yes. They haven't moved. The person is next to the fence by the front."

"Okay. You should be able to hear the sirens coming by now."

It was faint but Meghan could hear it. "Yes. I hear them."

She saw the red flashes cutting through the trees that lit up the area where the person had been. A tall figure took off in the opposite direction and Meghan raced to the front door to warn the officer. She met him on the porch, and she pointed in the direction the guy had gone. "He took off around the back of the house."

The officer nodded and shot around the side, disappearing in the darkness.

At least now she knew it was a man by his stature— a tall one, which meant it wasn't Rim. Who could it be, though? And what had he been planning?

She swallowed hard and wrapped her arms around her waist, the chill in the air causing goose bumps to form on her skin.

Here, she thought she was safe after Andrew's conversation. Now, she wasn't sure. Could it have been someone trying to steal something? If so, why stand by the trees for so long?

Meghan knew they were there for her and that left a sick feeling in her gut, one that she wasn't going to be able to dismiss.

The officer came back around the corner, his chest heaving in and out. "He got away," he said between breaths. "You said you heard a car door but there was no vehicle that I could see when I drove in."

"There's an old gravel drive off to the left of the main road. Maybe he parked there. It would be close enough to hear the slam from the house."

"I'll go look. Go inside and lock the door until I return."

Meghan did as she was told and walked into the kitchen to make some coffee. She wasn't getting any sleep tonight and she might as well have something to offer the deputy when he returned.

Ten minutes later, the coffee brewing, a knock on her door made her jump. She hated being scared again. Brooksville had been her salvation and now she had to worry about staying alone.

She went to open the door. "Anything?" Meghan asked, hoping he'd at least been able to get a plate number.

"Nope. I didn't see anything, though I could smell exhaust smoke in the air and a hint of something else I couldn't quite place."

Meghan sighed and allowed him into her house. "I made some coffee. Would you like a cup?"

"I'd love one. Thanks."

She led him to the kitchen and grabbed two cups from the cabinet and filled both to the brim. "Cream or sugar?"

"Black's fine."

She handed him one and went to lean against the farmhouse sink.

"Do you have any idea who it could have been?" he asked, taking a sip of his coffee.

"I thought I did at first, but once I got a closer look when they ran past the porch, there was no way it was him. This guy was too tall."

"I'll drink my coffee and go back to the cruiser and call this in. I'll stay here and keep an eye out until morning. You don't need to worry about him getting to you. Tomorrow, though, you may want to rethink your living arrangements. A single lady, staying so far out of town might not be for the best."

Just the thought of having to move out of a place she loved made Meghan furious. No way was she going to allow anyone to alter her life, not after her upbringing.

Nope. That'd been her life growing up and she'd never allow that to happen again. No one was going to have that kind of power over her.

She raised her chin in defiance and smiled. "I'll be fine."

"Suit yourself, but I think you should consider safety first."

Meghan knew he was probably right, that she should think about what he was saying, and maybe she would come morning, but right now she was angry, and she'd never made good decisions in that state. Perhaps, after a good night's sleep, she might think differently.

Chapter Six

Jake rubbed his eyes as they sat at the long table in the compounds dining area. He was trying to concentrate on the conversation with Andrew, Cullen, and one of the other men who he'd just met but was having trouble. Sleep had been nonexistent since he'd gotten there.

Hell, he didn't trust anyone, and that made it hard to relax enough to fall asleep.

"What do you think, Jackson?" Cullen asked, poking his ribs when he didn't answer.

Jake winced, and shrugged, not even sure what the man had asked. He needed to get his head in the game, or they'd probably rethink having him around.

He turned when he heard a laugh from behind him. Felix Rim stood in the food line, a plate in his hand, his attention on the redhead at his side. A woman he'd seen a few times in the kitchen. She ran a hand up the skinheads back and gave the man a provocative smile. The two had to have shared a sexual relationship and that relieved Jake. Now, hopefully, he'd stay away from Meghan.

"You need to stop glaring at Rim." Andrew shook his head. "Holding a grudge against anyone here doesn't work in my book. You need to get over this animosity real fast."

Under the table, Jake clenched his fists, intent on holding his tongue. No way was he ever going to forget what that scum ball had attempted to do to Meghan. That shit went beyond the pale, to the point that he'd never give Rim the time of day, no matter how much Andrew wanted him to. But Gibson didn't need to know that.

"You got nothing to say?" Andrew asked.

This was a test. Oh, how he'd love to fail it. Yet, he couldn't say what he wanted to. Not when his career was on the line. It wasn't like Meghan cared one way or the other. Last time he'd seen her, she'd given him the go-to-hell look anyway.

"I don't have any problems. Just trying to fit in," Jake lied, sucking down the last of his coffee. "Now, I need to go do the dishes. I'll see you later."

Unfortunately, he had to walk by the couple who had started toward the table.

Jake simply nodded and left the room. Being around Rim made him want to pound sand.

As he was entering the kitchen, something from behind slammed into the back of his head, sending him to his knees. When he recovered, he ran his fingers over his scalp, feeling a huge lump forming, blinking to try to block out the pain.

He saw Felix standing next to the door, holding a glass pitcher in his hand, swinging it like it was a baseball bat.

"What the…" Jake stumbled to his feet.

"Don't ever turn your back on me again, Jackass," Rim said, twisting around and leaving the room, laughing as he disappeared.

Jesus fucking Christ. He wanted to follow the little prick out there and beat the shit out of him, but that would only get him booted. And telling anyone about what had happened wouldn't be any better. Jake was just going to have to take the abuse, though, he'd get even somehow. But not today since he could already feel his head starting to pound.

He searched the kitchen cabinets for a pain reliever yet came up empty. He was going to have to go to town and get something, or he'd be in agony for the rest of the day.

First, he'd need to rinse and load all the dishes into the washer before he could leave.

An hour later, he sat in his SUV, staring at the large picture window in front of Strom's pharmacy. He knew he should go elsewhere but for some reason he'd been drawn to the place—drawn to the woman who worked there.

His head started to thump, and his vision blurred. Jake had never had a concussion. Was this what this was? He had no idea.

He opened the car door and shuffled slowly to the entrance of the pharmacy. Maybe they could help him decide if he needed to be checked or not.

Inside the store, the bright lights had him squinting and swallowing bile that worked its way up his throat. Damn it all to hell. He wanted to strangle Rim for doing this to him.

He saw Meghan before she noticed him. She was wearing that white smock she'd worn before, this time over a pink, cotton top and a pair of black slacks. Her shoulder-length, light-blonde hair was tucked behind her ears and there was a smudging of dark circles under her eyes like she had gotten much sleep either. He wondered why? Was it because of what Rim had done. Had that become a nightmare for her? The thought alone made Jake want to ring the guy's neck.

He stumbled toward her, his head throbbing like a bitch now.

"Hello," he said in a voice he hardly recognized, not sure how she'd react to him being in the store.

Meghan looked his way and frowned. "Are you okay?" She rushed toward him. "Here, come and sit down. You look white as a ghost."

Once Jake was seated, he inhaled a deep breath and closed his eyes.

"Lyle, can you come here?" he heard Meghan say, refusing to open his eyes to the bright glare.

"What do you need?" a man asked from far away.

Jake forced himself to open his eyes as an old man came toward him, his spectacled eyes widening.

"What seems to be the problem, young man?"

"Let's just say I rammed my head into a glass pitcher."

Both looked at him as if he'd lost his mind.

"Okay, someone wracked me in the head with a glass pitcher."

"Where?" the old man asked.

Jake raised his hand to the spot and winced. The pharmacist repeated the action.

"Could you close your eyes and reopen them?"

Jake didn't question why just did as instructed.

"I don't think you have a concussion, though you could visit the ER to be sure. I'd suggest acetaminophen. I'll get a bottle and some water so you can take some now. Every four hours or as needed take two more. No more than eight total a day. Can you remember that?"

Before he could reply, Meghan said, "I'll run and get it," She raced to the back of the store and returned with a bottle of water and a small, red box in her hand.

She quickly ripped open the container and extracted two tablets and handed them to him.

He popped both pills into his mouth and washed them down with the water.

"You need to stay awake for the rest of the day just to be on the safe side. If you feel nauseous, head straight to the ER. Understand?" the old man asked, his eyes intent on Jake.

Jake nodded, wincing when intense pain hit him again.

"Did you drive here?"

"I did."

"I suggest you don't again until you feel better, at least for a few days. Care to tell me who hit you in the head?"

Jake glanced at Meghan, who was watching him like a bird of prey. He wasn't going to say. Felix was a sore subject to be sure. He didn't want to bring him up now.

"I should go," he said, trying to rise, only to get dizzy and have to sit back down.

"You are in no shape to go anywhere alone, son." He placed a hand on Jake's shoulder and applied pressure. "I have an idea." The old man's face seemed to light up. "We're about to close for the day. Meghan here could take you home with her and keep an eye on you. That way, neither you, nor she, have to be alone tonight. Sounds like a good plan. Right? You are in no shape to do any harm. I'm not worried about that."

Meghan's jaw slackened. It was clear she didn't like the idea. Jake didn't much either, especially when she looked like she wanted to crawl in a hole and die.

"I'll be fine." Jake tried to get up again, only to be restrained.

"See, you'd be helping me out, young man. Meghan had a scare last night, and I really don't want her out in the middle of the boonies by herself right now. Two bird's kind of thing, you know. So, what do you say? I'll throw in the acetaminophen and bottled water for free."

Jake looked at Meghan. "Was it Felix?"

She shook her head. "I don't know who it was. But I'm almost certain it wasn't him."

"I'm not sure how much help I could be right now, but I will accept the proposal if you will. Just for tonight." It was stupid to agree. Jake knew that. Yet, her being in danger made the decision for him. He could be there to protect her. As best he could in his incapacitated state.

He glanced at her again. She didn't want to say yes. He could see it in her eyes—and her rigid stance. Would she defy her boss? Could she say no?

"All right. One night and you'll go back to your life, and I'll go back to mine. Is that clear?"

"Yes, ma'am."

"We are taking my car. You can lock up yours. The police patrol comes by periodically. No one should break into it overnight out front. Let me grab my stuff and I'll help you to the car. She turned to her boss. "We'll talk in the morning." There was an insinuation to her words that, that talk wouldn't be pleasant. Jake wouldn't want to be him, but again, he was going home with her. His time in the barrel might just be coming once they were alone. The thought had his head throbbing harder in his ears, so loud it hurt.

****

Meghan unlocked the front door and allowed Jackson inside. She wanted to skin Lyle alive. How dare he suggest she take a white supremacist home with her. The old man had lost his mind.

She led Jackson to the sofa and helped him sit. "How's your head? Has the acetaminophen helped any?"

"Well, I'm no longer wishing I was dead, so yeah, I feel better."

"Relax here. I'm going to run and change. Once I'm done, I'll see what I can fix for supper."

"Don't go to any trouble for me. I'm not all that hungry."

Meghan shrugged. "Maybe you'll change your mind later. Excuse me."

She rushed to her bedroom and closed the door, leaning against it. How had she gotten talked into this? Jackson was the last man she wanted in her home. He was no better than a Nazi yet looking at him was difficult. He was too good looking for her sanity. And she had to spend the evening with him. All night. Dusk till dawn. With him sleeping only a few feet away.

Meghan swallowed hard and moved, stripping off her top and slacks, tossing them onto the bed. She'd put them in the hamper in the bathroom later, once she got her head back on straight.

She dug through her dresser drawer and pulled out a pair of gray sweats and a white t-shirt. She was going to look as unappealing as she could. That way, neither would get any ideas.

When dressed, she tucked her work clothes under her arm and went to the bathroom and tossed them into the hamper, turning on the water to wash the makeup off her face.

She glanced in the mirror and smiled. The desired look. An almost thirty-year-old spinster with a face full of freckles wouldn't stir any desire in the man on her couch.

She dried off and left, thinking of what she could make for a meal. If he wasn't here, she might settle for a bowl of cereal or a bag of microwave popcorn but that wouldn't do. Not for him. The man needed a decent meal with meat and potatoes. Too bad she was a vegetarian. She did have an occasional egg or two. Maybe she'd make an omelet with some mushrooms and peppers. Easy to fix and filling enough for a man.

In the kitchen, she went to work. First, she'd put on a pot of coffee just in case Jackson would like some.

Fifteen minutes later, she placed everything on the table and walked into the living room, her heart instantly coming to a stop when she saw that Jackson's eyes were closed. She was supposed to keep him awake.

Please be all right.

"Jackson." She touched his arm.

He didn't respond. She shook him slightly and still nothing. Did she need to call for an ambulance? Meghan didn't know. What if he died? Could she live with herself?

Meghan turned away as tears filled her eyes. She bit down hard on her bottom lip, the taste of blood bringing her back to reality. She needed to do something. When she leaned in to see if he was breathing, his arm moved and accidentally brushing the side of her breast, causing her nipple to harden.

What the hell was wrong with her? The guy could be dying and here she was reacting to his touch.

"You okay?"

His question had her looking at him, his eyes now open, deep lines furrowing in his forehead.

"You scared me to death." She sucked in a cleansing breath. "I couldn't wake you. I thought…"

"I'm okay, Meghan." He cupped her cheek with his hand.

The action sent her heart racing in her chest. She found herself staring into his hypnotic eyes, couldn't move even if she wanted to. He had her caught in his intoxicating stare.

He leaned toward her and was about to kiss her when she remembered what he was—a hate-filled man who hung around like-minded people and she abruptly moved away. "Dinner is ready. It's not much. But you need to try to eat something." She swirled on her heels and raced to the kitchen, scolding herself the whole way.

Had she lost her mind? Apparently. Why else would she come that close to kissing him?

One thing was for sure, she couldn't trust her actions around the man, and it was best, after tonight, to never be left alone with him again.

Chapter Seven

A noise from somewhere woke Jake out of a deep sleep and forced him to blink several times to clear his vision. He eased to a sitting position on the couch and combed his hands through his hair, accidentally bumping the knot on his head.

Shit, that's going to hurt for a while.

He looked around, inhaling deeply when he heard creaking, not from inside the house but possibly on the front porch.

Jake rose, teetering left to right, fighting his equilibrium.

Damn it all to hell.

He was going to get Rim back once his story was written. It was a dirty shot to hit someone from behind. Felix was going to pay for that whack ten times over.

Another squeaking floorboard brought him back to his dilemma. Someone was sneaking around outside, like Strom had insinuated the night before, and part of the reason as to why he was here.

He shuffled to the front door and glanced out the window but couldn't see anything. Maybe it was just a raccoon or an opossum scavenging for food. He'd seen a lot of them down this way, especially around wooded areas.

Jake was about to leave the window when he caught sight of a shadow off to the right of the porch. He stayed still and watched as the person leaned forward and look into a window that had to be Meghan's bedroom. Was this some sick peeping tom? Who the hell watched a woman sleep? Fucking Felix Rim. That's who.

Angry, he looked around for something to use on the intruder and came up empty. He had to do something. He couldn't allow the guy to continue to watch her.

He slid the bolt lock open and turned the doorknob, hoping to get a jump on the prowler. He eased the door open, all the while watching to see if the shadow moved. As he stepped outside, the person watching Meghan turned, the whites of his eyes widening.

Jake scrambled toward him, grabbing ahold of the guy's arm, keeping him from getting away. The two scuffled until Jake twisted the man's arm behind his back. The action rattled his brain, causing his head to pound again.

"What's going on?" Meghan came rushing toward him, a bat held in one of her hands.

"This guy was peeping through your window?" He shoved him forward. "You know him?"

She moved closer and her eyes widened. "Daddy? What are you doing here?"

"He's your father?" Jake instantly loosened his grip but didn't release him.

"How did you find me?"

For God sakes, she'd taken Jake in and cared for him while he was recovering and this is the thanks he'd given her—man-handling her dad. Would she send him packing now? In the dark? Jake was a city boy, not used to traipsing around the countryside at night. Who knew what he'd run into out here.

"I'm sorry. I didn't know he was your father." Jake

noticed the deep frown line on Meghan's forehead. She didn't seem happy to see her dad. Jake wondered if he should let him go or not.

"So, no hug for your old man?" the gray-haired guy asked.

She hesitated for a moment and looked annoyed as she wrapped her arms around him for a brief second and quickly stepped away.

"What are you doing here? Where's Momma?"

"Your mother doesn't know I'm here. She would've tried to talk me out of coming."

Jake could see Meghan's discomfort—knew she wasn't thrilled about her father's visit, but he had caught a whiff of the man's breath when they'd tussled. Alcohol was present. Was that why she wasn't all that happy to see him?

"What do you want, Daddy?"

"Aren't you going to invite me in and introduce me to your husband here."

"Wait, I—"

Meghan cut him off. "How did you get here? I know you don't have a license anymore."

"License, smicence. I can drive when I want. I don't need a stupid card to do that."

"So, you have Momma's car? How's she going to get to work tomorrow?"

"She can call one of her friends to drive her. She don't need the car all the time. Are you going to let me inside or not?"

"I think you should start for home. Momma's going to need the car early in the morning."

"Stop talking about the dumb car." He brushed past them and walked toward the door. "I guess I'll just invite myself in, little girl."

Jake watched until he entered the house and glanced back at Meghan. "I take it you aren't thrilled to see him?"

"Not even a little. Look, I need to ask a favor."

"Okay. What's that?"

"I don't have time to explain now, but you have to pretend to be my husband until he leaves."

"Wait, what?"

"Just follow my lead, okay. He'll leave come morning and the charade will be over. I just need you to do this for me. Okay?"

Jake wasn't sure what to say. No one had ever asked to marry him—faux or not. This was a first.

"This won't get out, right?"

"Look, Jackson, I don't want to do this any more than you do, but my father will leave me alone if he thinks I'm married. He'll realize he no longer has control over my life. Can you just go along with me on this?"

The desperate look she gave him was his undoing. "Sure, okay."

"Come on. Before he steals the silverware."

"Sounds like a great guy."

She snorted, leaving Jake to wonder how a caring woman like Meghan had a father with a handful of vices.

He started for the door. As long as he and Meghan's nuptials were make-believe and stayed that way, there was no harm in him playing along. After all, hadn't she helped him when he'd needed her. This was the least he could do.

****

Meghan knew she had to play this right or life as she'd known it the past year would be over. Her father had to go, and she'd do anything to achieve that.

She stepped into the house and glanced around, not seeing him. Where had he gone? She rushed to the kitchen where she found him going through her refrigerator.

"I don't have anything to drink, Daddy."

He slammed the door and glared at her. "Didn't I teach you anything?"

"Actually, yes. You taught me not to drink alcohol."

"Phfft, you're just like your mother. Always walking around with a stick up your ass."

Meghan clenched her fists tightly. The man had some nerve telling her she was strait-laced. He expected her to live like a nun, no sex before marriage, no going out with anyone who wasn't a member of the church he was deacon of. Yet, his drinking excessively wasn't a problem. Such a religious hypocrite.

"What is it you really want?"

"Can't a father want to see his baby girl?"

"Why? What do you need?"

"I want to know why you left your mother and me. Up and disappeared in the middle of the night? Did you come to Brooksville with this guy?" He pointed toward Jackson, who was leaning his shoulder against the doorframe, watching their exchange.

"No. I came here alone and met Jackson."

"How long you two been married?"

"Not long," she said, hoping Jackson would simply nod in agreement. The less talking he did, the better off they'd be.

"What do you do for a living, young man?"

Meghan didn't expect her father to ask that question. What was Jackson going to say? Hopefully, not the truth.

"I little of this and that."

"What does that mean?"

Jackson stuffed a hand into the front of his jeans pocket. "I find work where I can. Like a freelancer."

"So, Meghan is supporting you?"

"No, Daddy. I think you're thinking of Momma, who has supported you for the past fifteen years. Since you have that back injury." *A fake back injury.*

"You need to have some respect for your old man, girlie. Now, since you ain't got anything to drink, show me where I can sleep."

"You'll be sleeping on the couch. I only have one bedroom."

She walked toward the door, sidling past Jackson.

In the living room, she stared at the bedding, hoping her father wouldn't assume anything.

"Looks like somebody's already sleepin' on the couch. Trouble in paradise?" her father asked, eyeing her intently.

"Not at all," Jackson cut in before Meghan could say anything. "Fell asleep watching a movie."

The old man seemed skeptical for a moment, then shrugged and sat down onto the couch. "Well, goodnight."

Meghan looked at Jackson. "Okay. Goodnight."

She grasped his arm and pulled him to her bedroom. Inside, after securing the door, she glanced back at him, unsure what to do now. She really hadn't thought this plan though. She didn't have any extra blankets or pillows. They were being used on the couch by her father, and it was much too cold for Jackson to sleep on the floor. Which meant they were going to have to share the bed.

She glanced back up at him and noticed his eyes had

become glassy. He was in pain. How could she have forgotten that he could have a concussion?

In a whisper, she said, "Let's get into bed and get some rest."

He didn't argue. Just headed for the bed, which meant he was suffering. She'd really like to know how he'd gotten the blow to the head, yet that wasn't her biggest concern. That was, once they were lying next to each other, would she be able to fall asleep?

"What side do you sleep on?"

"The right side," she answered going to get in on that side.

He got in on the other and tucked his arm under his pillowless head and got comfortable.

"I want to thank you for helping me."

"It's okay, Meghan. I get that you and your father don't see eye-to-eye."

She rolled to her side to face him. "That's an understatement. Daddy's a religious zealot with a drinking problem. And yes, I know that doesn't sound right, but in DeWitt County, men rule over the women and can do whatever they want. The females have a set of rules to follow. I left because I was going to be forced to marry someone I couldn't stand. The most conceited ass who was a philandering, misogynist lout with delusions of grandeur."

"Sounds like a catch," he said with a smirk.

She smiled back. "Truly."

"How did you end up in Brooksville?"

"I packed a bag and waited until dark, hitched a ride out of town and never looked back. I've never been happier. I learned to rely on myself. I like being able to live on my own. Not needing a man for anything."

"Does that mean you're into...well...you know."

Meghan frowned. "What?"

"Are you a ...into, you know...women?"

"Oh, because I said I didn't need a man for *anything*. I get it. No. I'm not a lesbian. Though, even if I was, I wouldn't have time for a relationship. I work too many hours."

He turned on his side. "You know what they say about all work and no play."

She frowned. "No. What do they say?"

"Hmmm...I'm not really sure what they say." He squinted as he looked at her. "Could you turn out that light on the table? The glare's hurting my eyes."

"Of course." She flipped off the switch. "Do you need me to get another acetaminophen or two?"

"I think if I just close my eyes, I'll feel better."

"Are you sure? Maybe I should watch you in case you do have a concussion."

"I don't think I do. The dizziness is gone now. I just have a dull ache where I was hit. I think I'll be fine."

"If you are sure."

He smiled. "I am."

"Okay. Good night, Jackson."

"Night."

Meghan rolled to her back and stared at the ceiling. If Jackson wasn't a member of that hateful group, she'd like him. But he was, so she needed to keep her distance. Funny, since he was lying next to her in bed. Tomorrow though, he'd be gone and she could go back to avoiding him like the plague.

Chapter Eight

Jake eased open his eyes, while trying to figure out what was weighing on his chest. It took a moment for his vision to clear and he glanced down to find a creamy-white arm draped across his pecs. Meghan's.

He turned his head. She was facing him, her eyes closed, looking too beautiful for her own good. And his. Something about this woman appealed to Jake in a realm of different ways. Her past only amplified that. When she'd told him how her father had wanted her to marry a man she didn't love, it'd stirred a protectiveness inside him. No woman should have to go through something like that. It wasn't the fifties. Weren't we way beyond arranged marriages? Apparently, not in this case.

He reached over and brushed his finger across her arm, her skin so soft and supple to the touch. She moved next to him, her fingers thrust between the buttons on his shirt, twining into the hairs on his chest, causing blood to surge to a certain body part. *Jesus Christ.*

Jake needed to cool his jets. He gently moved her arm, rose, and went to the bathroom. He needed some cold water to shock his system. Thank God he didn't have to pretend to be Meghan's husband much longer. Not when he'd now have a hard time controlling his body around her.

Once he'd cooled his face with ice cold water, he dried off and reopened the bathroom door to find

Meghan up, rifling through her dresser.

"We need to hurry. I must be to work in an hour."

"I just need to throw on my boots," he said, walking around the bed. "What are you going to do about your father?"

"I'm going to get him to leave. He can't stay here. He'll steal something."

"You want me to get rid of him while you're getting ready for work. After all, I am your husband." He gave her a lopsided grin.

She snorted and stopped to look at him. "You can give it a try. It might work."

Jake looked down by the side of the bed for his boots, suddenly remembering he'd left them next to the couch. Hopefully, him insisting that the man leave would be enough to get him to go, otherwise, what was Meghan going to do? Stay here and watch him all day.

"Wish me luck. I'm going in," he said and opened the door to find the man wasn't on the couch. Maybe he'd gone to the kitchen to make coffee, though Jake didn't smell any brewing.

He came up short in the kitchen. Perhaps he'd headed home. That would be preferable for Meghan.

Jake stepped back into the living room to find his boots, yet all he saw were a pair of beat-up tennis shoes. Wow. Did that mean the man stole his Stetsons? A pair of black leather biker boots that he'd paid a pretty penny for. To add insult to injury, the shoes that were left were two sizes smaller than his feet.

He plopped down onto the sofa and leaned back and closed his eyes. What kind of person stole a pair of boots that were too big for them?

"Did your headache come back?" Meghan asked.

"Nope. I'm fine." Jake had to remember it wasn't her fault her father was a piece of shit.

"Where's my daddy?"

"I don't know. I couldn't find him or my boots."

"What?"

"I left my boots out here last night and all I found weren't these sneakers." He picked them up to show her.

She came around the couch to look at him, her eyes brimming with unshed tears. "So, Daddy took your boots and left those?"

"Appears so, yes. The kicker, my boots are two sizes bigger than these. I couldn't wear them if I wanted to."

"Were your boots expensive?"

"Let's just say they weren't cheap."

A single tear slipped down her cheek. "I'll pay you back, Jackson."

"You don't have to do that. You can't control your father and what he does."

"I know but I still want to get you another pair. You have to let me."

Jake wasn't going to argue with her. She looked mortified by her father's theft.

"Sure. But don't run out now. I have another pair of boots at the compound. So, there's no hurry."

"I just feel wretched. I should have told you to get them. I wasn't thinking."

Jake shrugged. "They're just boots, Meghan. It's not important to me. I'm just glad that your intruder was your father and not Rim."

She swiped at her eyes and nodded in agreement. "I never did thank you for helping me that day. That encounter was so ugly."

"No man should ever treat a woman like that."

His comment earned him a weak smile, one that he was grateful for. Meghan was too sweet to be sad. She seemed like a genuinely kind person. There weren't many of those anymore. His mother. His sister. Her.

Jake shook the thought. For some reason, he was lumping her in with his family. She wasn't part of that. He barely knew her.

"Are you ready to go?" he asked, thinking it was best to part ways as soon as possible. She was making him think outrageous things and that was not why he was here. Jake had a story to write. He needed to focus on that.

Her eyes narrowed, yet she smiled and said, "Yes. I am."

Jake walked to the front door, ready to pad carefully to the car in his stocking feet. He had sensitive soles. This was going to be interesting.

Meghan raced to her bedroom and returned with her purse and keys. She was heading for the front door right when it opened and in walked her father, two grocery bags clutched in each hand.

"What are you doing back?" she asked him, the look on her face grim.

"I went into town to get some groceries." He lifted his arms to show her. "You didn't have much."

"How did you pay for these groceries, Daddy? Jackson couldn't find his boots this morning. Any idea what happened to them?"

The older man shrugged. "What are you insinuating, little girl?"

The fake indignation had Jake inwardly smiling and looking down at the man's feet. He wore a new pair of sneakers. It was clear the man lied on cue. He deserved an award.

"Did you hock his boots?" Meghan asked, her eyes piecing her father's.

"I didn't take his damned boots. Now, I'm going to go fix me some breakfast. You want some, you're going to have to apologize first." He walked away without so much as a backwards glance.

Bravo. Quite the performance.

"So, what are you going to do now? He's making himself at home."

Meghan shook her head and frowned. "I don't know. I have to get to work. Lyle can't run the pharmacy alone."

"You want me to stay and keep an eye on him?" Jake had no idea why he'd made the offer. He had places to be, people to investigate. Yet, Meghan looked desperate.

"I can't ask you to do that, Jackson."

"You didn't. I offered." He pointed to the door. "Now, go. You are going to be late. I'll see that he doesn't steal anything else."

"Thank you. I'll be back at 5:30."

"We'll be here," Jake reassured her of that with a wink.

She left and Jake sucked in a calming breath. *God.* This was not how he'd planned to spend his day—babysitting an old man who lied and stole at will—two of the things his father had taught him not to do. That fact made him appreciate William Mills even more.

****

Meghan finished up the sweeping and threw the debris into the wastebasket and placed the broom and pan back into the storage room. All day she'd worried about Jackson—how he'd fared. Her father was difficult on a good day. She could only imagine how hard it had been for someone who'd never experienced him before.

"I'll lock up, Meghan. You get on home and see what's left of it." Lyle shook his finger in the air.

"Thanks. I'll see you in the morning."

Meghan rushed to get the cheap tennis shoes she'd bought for Jackson and raced to the car, nervous about what she'd find once she returned home. Would he forgive her for placing him in such a precarious situation?

Again though, he was a member of a hate group. He could surely handle her father.

It took her ten minutes to get home. A record. As she opened her car door and grabbed her bags, Jackson stepped out the front door and smiled.

Her heart fluttered and instantly accelerated at a breakneck speed. What was it about this man that caused her to lose her senses? She didn't know but she needed to regain them quickly since he was off limits.

"How was your day?" he asked once she'd stepped up onto the porch.

"Fine. How was yours?"

He cocked his head to the side and grinned. "Let's just say it was interesting."

She stared intently at him. "Care to elaborate?"

"Maybe later. Suppers on the table."

Shock would have been a mild word for how Meghan felt by what he'd said. "Who fixed the meal?" There were only two things her father could cook, and neither were appetizing.

"I did. Is that all right?"

He opened the door and allowed her inside. Meghan looked around, noting how clean the place looked.

"You've been busy," she said.

"It was either stay busy or listen to your father regale me with stories of how he walked on water."

She snorted. "Yeah, I should have warned you about that before I left."

He heaved a sigh. "It was best you didn't. I would have changed my mind about staying."

"I appreciate your sacrifice. Where is he?"

"He's in the kitchen. He refused to wait for you, and he's on his fourth whisky and coke."

"Of course, he is. One more and he'll pass out. The man had half his stomach removed. He can't drink like he used to."

"Good to know."

Meghan entered the kitchen, not at all surprised to see her father slumped over his empty plate. Drunk as usual. Nothing in the year she'd been here had changed him. Still a waste of space.

"Want to help me get him to the couch?" she asked Jackson, feeling her cheeks redden. The man was an embarrassment.

"Let me do it." He walked to the table. "You've had a long day."

"I'd prefer mine to yours," she shot back, pulling the half empty glass out of her father's grip.

Jackson hefted her father up and dragged him from the kitchen. A moment later he returned. "He's all tucked in for the night. So, you said he only has half a stomach. What happened?"

Meghan sighed. "Cancer. Four years ago."

"You're lucky you still have him. I wasn't myself. Now, sit and I'll get the food on the table."

Everything about Jackson was a contradiction to

Meghan. How could someone who seemed kind and thoughtful belong to a hate group? It didn't make any sense.

Jackson placed a plate in front of her, along with a casserole dish filled with a bubbly, tomato and cheesy lasagna. He left again and returned with a garden salad with ranch dressing. "Did I have this in my refrigerator?" she asked, almost positive she didn't.

"Nope. Your father and I went into the store. I promised to buy him a bottle of Jack if he went inside first to buy me some shoes." He pointed to the black tennis shoes he wore. Meghan hadn't even noticed them.

"How much do I owe you?"

He sat across from her. "You don't owe me anything, Meghan. Now, let's eat before it gets cold."

Meghan cut a large slice and placed one on his plate, another on hers. It was nice to come home and have something filling. Not like what she usually fixed. Everything about having him here was nice, but she couldn't get used to that. No matter how helpful he was, he still represented something she couldn't abide. Once her father was gone, so would he be, and that was that. There was no playing house with Jackson. End of story.

Chapter Nine

While they ate supper, Jake found himself totally engrossed with Meghan and their conversation. For a woman with no formal education, she appeared to be well read. He'd learned she hadn't gone to college, though her mother's work at the local high school had opened avenues of learning for Meghan. With her spending long hours in the library as she waited for her mother to finish work. According to her, it was either that or being at home with her drunken father. In Jake's eyes, she chose wisely.

"What about you?" she asked as she cleared the table. "Did you go to college?"

Jake had slipped up early by saying he hadn't been so lucky about the cancer thing. He needed to stay on script. He was Jackson Gallagher, not Jake Mills. Even with her.

"I didn't, no."

"At least you don't have all that student debt, right?"

He wished he could tell her the truth, but he couldn't. It was too dangerous for him. She might tell the wrong people.

"That is one way to look at it."

She filled the sink with water and squeezed in some dish soap. "It's not too late for either of us, though, you know. Lyle wants me to take over the pharmacy one day. Yet, all that schooling scares me."

"I think you should. Let me help you with those." Jake brought the rest of the dishes to her. "You wash, I'll dry."

"Thank you, Jackson, for everything."

He shrugged. "I'm glad I could help."

"I don't suppose my daddy told you how long he'd be staying?"

"Nope. I did hint, though, that he should head home soon."

She gave him a weak smile. "What did he say to that?"

Jake grinned back. "To mind my own business. That we had the rest of our lives to be lovey-dovey. Oh, and he winked at me and told me he wants some grandbabies soon."

Her cheeks turned bright red, and she fumbled with the dish she was washing. "Look, Jackson, I don't expect you to continue to play along with this ruse. The whole thing was stupid. I know you have your own life to live."

Jake studied her closely, knew Meghan meant every word. She hated having to pretend with him. But after spending the day with her father, he could see why she'd done it. The man was a narcissist. "I'm here Meghan because I want to be. I'm in no hurry to get back to my life." Not entirely untrue. Yes, he had a story to write, yet he was in no rush to see Rim again. He wasn't sure he could control his need to beat the man within an inch of his life after what he'd done. Best to stay away and cool his jets. At least, for a few days.

She held out a clean plate for him to dry. "Are you sure?"

He took the slippery dish and ran the towel over the top. "Yes, now let's drop the subject and get these dishes done."

"Okay." She smiled again. This time the gesture looked genuine and sent his heart racing in his chest.

Shit. If a smile could cause such a reaction, what was going to happen when he was once again in bed with her? Alone. Her warm body next to his.

Sweat formed on his upper lip. He quickly swiped it away with his sleeve.

"Is your head hurting again," she asked looking concerned.

Was his sexual frustration so apparent she'd thought he was in pain? He was in a way since the head of his fucking cock hurt.

He was going to need to take a cold shower before bed. Otherwise, he'd suffer a restless, agonizing night.

Once they'd finished dishes and got everything put away, he left the kitchen, hoping distance and some cool night air would help douse the fire burning inside his gut.

He stepped onto the porch and took in a long, cleansing breath. No woman had ever caused such a reaction before, and it didn't make sense. He barely knew her. But the chemistry was undeniable. Yet that was all it could ever be since he wasn't into simple sex for release. Jake was raised better than that. And, with him not staying in town and living hours away from Brooksville, what kind of future could the two share? The whole idea was futile. His body needed to remember that—too bad it hadn't been satisfied for some time, which only made things worse.

If he knew his way around the countryside, he'd go for a long run, but he didn't. He'd have to settle with that cold shower instead and hope that'd be enough.

Back inside the house, he glanced at the couch,

shaking his head at the old man snoring away. All day he'd followed Jake around, a glass of booze in his hand, spouting off about how the Lord was okay with him abiding of liquor—that Jesus loved his wine and drank often. Jake didn't question that, though he had his own opinion on the matter. He'd learned from years on the job, you could justify anything if you wanted it badly enough. Jake could see why Meghan ran away even without her impending nuptials. The man was a charlatan.

He turned away and noticed Meghan's bedroom door stood open. He strode to the entrance and ducked his head inside. The bathroom door was closed, and he heard the shower running.

Jake forced a lump in his throat down. She was inside, naked, water cascading over her delectable body.

Yeah. This is going to be a great night.

His mouth went dry, and he turned around and headed for the kitchen to get a drink. At the sink, he ran the stream of water into a tall glass and gulped it down, watching shadows from the wind playing through the row of fir trees. This part of Missouri was quite beautiful, though isolated for a city boy. He was used to the nightlife. Going out to eat every night at some place someone recommended, Halloweens spent with a group of his best friends at Lemp Mansion, searching for ghosts at the bewitching hour. This was the complete opposite. At least Andrew's compound was on the edge of town, somewhat less detached than this.

He poured another glass of water, gulped it down, stuck the glass inside the sink and went back to Meghan's room. She was already in bed, reading a book, a cute little pair of readers perched on her delicate nose.

"Care if I take a quick shower?" he asked when she looked up.

"Not at all. Take your time." She sighed and went back to reading the book in her hands.

Jake closed himself off in the bathroom. He was going to take his time. Because once he was in bed next to her, his body was going to revolt, and he needed time to prepare for that fact.

****

Meghan's eyes started to feel heavy, and she placed the mystery novel she was reading on the side table, took off her glasses and set them next to the book. When she was about to doze off, the other side of the bed creaked and dipped. She caught herself before rolling into him. She'd almost forgotten the two would be sharing a bed again. How was she going to fall asleep now, especially since he was fresh out of a shower, smelling so good?

She turned to her side, facing the wall, intent on ignoring his presence. After all, she had to work early and needed the rest.

Minute by agonizing minute ticked by like each were an hour as pictures of Jackson flashed before her eyes. What would he look like with no shirt? Did he have a hairy chest? Meghan liked that. *Right. Like you've seen a man's chest in real life.*

Her upbringing had been too sheltered, and once she escaped, she didn't have time to find out. Maybe that time was now? Perhaps Jackson could help her out with that pesky virginity thing. What did she need it for anyway? It wasn't like she had to save herself any longer for marriage. Why not just get that out of the way? Tonight.

She rolled onto her back and glanced at him. He had

71

his back to her, the blue T-shirt he'd worn now for two days stretched taut across his shoulders. She should have gotten him another shirt. What would her daddy think of him not changing his clothes. Would he think the two were lying to him about being married?

Meghan shook off the thought. This was not the time to be thinking about her father, not when she wanted Jackson to have sex with her.

"Are you still awake?" she asked just above a whisper.

"Yep," he said, not turning over.

"Can I ask you something?"

"What's that?" Still, he refused to look at her.

"Could you roll over, please?"

"Do I have to?" His voice sounded throaty. Like he was in pain. That concerned her. "Is your head bothering you again?"

"Yes, but not the one you think."

Meghan sat up in bed. "I don't understand."

"Never mind. What kind of favor did you want?"

She reached over and touched his arm, a gesture that he pulled away from. "Did I do something to upset you?"

He turned to look at her. "You didn't do anything, Meghan. It's just hard to be here, in your bed."

"Why?" she asked, though it was starting to register that the two might be on the same page with their thoughts. Good. It would make it easier if he was into her as well. Though, there would have to be ground rules between them. Tonight, would be it. No return visits. No relationship. Just the end to her virginity.

"It's harder for a man to control certain urges. Do you get what I'm saying?"

"Sexual urges?"

"Yes. That. Now, let's go to sleep."

"About those sexual urges."

He made a repressed sound that brought a smile to her face. "You think this is funny?"

"Ask me what the favor was again."

"What? Are you playing some kind of game, Meghan? If so, I don't like it. I told you this was hard for me."

"Could you please shut up for a moment and just listen?" He was about to say something yet instead closed his mouth.

Meghan looked him in the eye. "I have this little problem I'd like you to take care of for me."

"What problem in that?"

"You know how I told you about my life growing up. How my daddy was trying to marry me off?"

"Yeah."

"Well, to do that sanctioned by the church, the woman must be chaste. Do you understand what I'm saying?"

His eyes widened when the realization hit him. "So, you were a virgin?"

"Yes, and still am. I'd like you to help me with that."

His eyes widened. "Wait, what?"

"I know it's a lot to ask. But I don't expect anything further. Okay?"

He stared at her as if she'd lost her mind, his mouth opening then closing again. He wanted to say something but thought better of it.

What did he want to tell her? Meghan wanted to know.

"Are you at least considering my request?"

He grimaced.

"What? Is the prospect that awful? I thought you were attracted to me."

"I am but—"

"But what?" she snapped. What kind of man would turn down such an offer? It wasn't like Jackson was some upstanding person in society. He was part of a hate group for God sakes.

"You know, forget I asked." Meghan pushed the covers aside.

He grasped her arm before she got out of bed. "I'm sorry, Meghan. This is a first for me, okay? I've never been asked to take anyone's innocence before. If this is what you want, I'll do it. But you need to be sure."

She sighed. "I wouldn't have asked if I wasn't."

"You do remember that your father is in the next room, right?"

"Passed out. There is no waking him when that happens. Believe me."

He stared at her for a long, agonizing moment. "Okay. I'm at your service. Do you want me to kiss you first?"

"I want you to take off your shirt. Can you do that?"

He nodded as he pulled the Tee over his head and tossed it on the floor, revealing curly, dark hair that peppered his pecs and led a trail from his belly button down to the waistband of his jeans. He was all sinewy muscle that more than fascinated her. Without thinking, she touched his chest, twining her fingers through the coarse hair, causing him to draw in a breath. It intrigued her that she could stir such a reaction from him. She continued her quest, gently palming her hand over his shoulder, up around his neck, drawing him in, her mouth now close to his. His warm breath heated her cheek and caused a strange tightening in her belly. She'd never experienced anything like it. Even the man she was engaged to, who she'd kissed on a few occasions had never made her feel this way. When his mouth came down onto hers, light at first, her world came crashing in around her. The more he kissed her the more she wanted him to, urging him on, opening her mouth, hoping he'd advance. His tongue slipped in and teased her own, heightening her senses, causing her breathing to labor.

Jackson abruptly drew back, and she felt disappointed until he clasped the hem of her shirt and pulled it over her head. She was naked underneath and he stared at her, the intensity in his gaze making her suddenly shy.

Instinctively, Meghan covered her breasts with her hands, only to have him push them away and pull her to him, the skin-on-skin connection electric. The hair on his chest caused an odd friction that excited her more. She could no longer focus on one thing. She needed to stay in control even though a throbbing sensation had started to build between her legs. Nothing she's experienced had been this intense, so mind-altering. Like something was going to happen that she'd never return from.

He eased her down into the mattress and laid half on top of her, his lips crushing hers, this time with demand, like he was on a mission. What that was, she hadn't a clue.

His hand slid up her ribcage and cupped one of her breasts, her nipple instantly beading and tingling. She arched her back, wanting more, yet unsure of what. Everything was new to her. Every prickle. Every muscle reaction. She didn't know what to do, how to respond.

His mouth left hers again and slid across her jawline,

inching slowly down her neck. Her skin erupted into a series of goosebumps.

Oh, God. What was happening to her.

She cupped his head and laced her fingers through the shafts of his hair, wanting him closer. His tongue flicked over her breast, the shock of it making her jerk, the heat of his mouth drawing up her nipple.

Meghan sucked in air, her legs flailing restlessly under the covers. He moved on to the other nipple, his hand cupping the other, and thumbing the tip.

Everything had gone full tilt in her brain as she relished the sensations. Right when she thought she was about to lose her mind, his hand left her breast and slid down her belly, under the elastic waistband of her pajama bottoms. Brazenly, he touched her where no one had before.

Was she really doing this? Could she allow him to be this intimate with her? When his finger delved inside her core, thought of anything but what he was doing vanished. All she could think about was the strange feeling that was building, like a storm brewing outside with the intensity of a category-5 tornado. Without a word, he stripped off his jeans, retrieved something from his wallet, and tore a foiled packet with his mouth and moments later covered her body with his, his weight only intensifying her stream of consciousness.

"Are you sure you want me to do this?" he asked in her ear.

"Yes."

He hesitated still, the thrum of his racing heartbeat notable in his throat. Maybe he was having second thoughts.

She reached up and brushed her finger against his

jaw and he groaned.

"If you at any time want me to stop, please say so."

She nodded and shimmied out of her bottoms and wrapped her arm around his neck and drew him in for a kiss—that was all the incentive he needed to proceed. He kneed her legs apart and eased between them, A sharp twinge sidelined her as he thrust inside.

"Are you okay?" he asked in an unrecognizable voice.

Meghan wasn't sure, yet responded with, "Yes. I'm fine."

He started to move in and out of her, slow and deliberate until that strange tension returned, building in intensity until she rose to meet his thrust. Suddenly, in an array of twinkling lights, her body exploded in release—something so overwhelming that it brought tears to her eyes. On top of her Jackson grunted and dropped onto her and rolled them both to his side and lay still, breathless.

She stole a glance at him, in total wonder at what had just happened to her. One thing was for sure. Only once wasn't going to be enough. That might have been the initial plan, yet now that she knew what her friends had been talking about the past year, all of it was flying straight out the window.

Chapter Ten

Jake awoke, feeling more relaxed than he'd been since he had lost his job. Meghan was the reason. Not only had he taken her virginity, but he'd also spent half the night between those lush thighs, giving and receiving pleasure.

He rolled over, eager to see her, only to find the bed empty. He glanced at the bathroom. The door was open, the light off. Maybe she was in the kitchen with her father.

With an eagerness he hadn't felt in a long time, he shoved the covers aside and rose, grabbing his clothes from the floor on the way to the bathroom to shower.

It was going to be hard to leave now, but the guns Rim had at the compound worried him. What could he be planning to do with them?

In the shower, Jake quickly washed his hair and body. After he turned off the water, he got out and toweled off. He wished he had another T-shirt to put on since he'd been wearing the same one for days.

When he stepped from the bathroom, he found Meghan standing next to the bed, holding a plastic bag in her hand.

"Good morning," he said, coming toward her.

"I ran into town and got you a few things. I didn't want daddy to wonder why you hadn't changed your clothes. I checked your stuff for sizes." She held out the bag.

He took it from her. "Thank you."

"Oh, and I got you a toothbrush and some other things you might need."

"Can I pay you for them."

"No. It's the least I can do. Now, I'm going to go fix us some breakfast before I have to leave for work."

Jake watched her go, admiring that cute little butt of hers. It was going to be hard saying goodbye. He was enjoying his time with her.

He reached into the bag and tore the tags from the articles of clothing and went to change and brush his teeth. That was the one thing he'd really missed, though he'd used his fingers to brush them the day before. Once he was finished, he left the room to find Meghan. He was going to have to spend another day with her father— something he was not looking forward to. Maybe he could convince him to go home today. That was going to be his goal, even if that meant he'd have to go back to the compound. And he could see Meghan on his off time.

He walked to the kitchen to find her standing in front of the stove, frying some bacon in a pan. He went to get a cup of coffee, in need of a little caffeine after his night with her. Why didn't she look even remotely tired?

"You need help?" he asked, sidling up next to her.

"I'm good. Take a seat. It'll be done in a few minutes."

"I didn't see your dad on the couch. Did he leave?"

She shook her head. "He's outside puking his guts out. That's also what he does after a day of drinking."

Jake frowned. "How long has he been doing this?"

She cocked her head to glance at him. "After he hurt his back. About ten years now."

"Has he tried to quit?"

"No. He doesn't think it's a problem."

He'd been fortunate to have the father he had. Some people weren't so lucky. Meghan seemed to be one of them.

"What about your parents? What are they like?"

Jake was going to have to lie to her again. He really hated that, especially after what they'd shared. He shrugged. "Never knew them. I was raised in foster care. Had a lot of stand-ins."

"I'm sorry." She gave him a look that made him want to slink away. Lying to her was agony. If she found out the truth, would she forgive him? Would he be able to if the tables were turned? Probably not.

"I lived through it."

She turned back to cooking.

Jake would love to know what she was thinking right now, but he wasn't going to ask. Best to drop the subject and not get in any deeper.

"I need a drink," her father said, bursting into the back door, looking almost green.

"Of coffee." Meghan graced the man with a look that Jake would've been intimidated by.

"Girlie, you need to lose your attitude."

She poured a cup of coffee and handed it to him. "This is my house, Daddy, and I'll speak the way I want to. Now, sit down and drink that coffee. If you're good, I'll make you some breakfast."

He mumbled something inaudible and slumped into a chair. With a grunt, he took a swallow of coffee, his grimace suggesting to Jake that he burned his mouth. It was going to be a long day if he couldn't get the man to leave.

The old man's attention turned to him. He grinned like a fool. "You two were awful noisy last night," he said in a low tone to keep Meghan from hearing. So much for the man being dead to the world like she'd assumed. Thank God he thought the two were married, otherwise he'd probably insist they get hitched.

Jake ignored him and sipped his coffee. Meghan placed a plate in front of him and another for her father, moments later returning to get herself a coffee and food.

When she sat down, Jake couldn't help but smile at the look of distaste she gave her dad. Her expression said it all. She had no respect for the man and Jake could hardly blame her. He'd only just met him, and he found him less than likable.

"You'll be happy to know, girlie, I'll be headed home today. Your momma will be missing me by now."

"I'm sure she is, Daddy. Tell her hello for me."

"You should tell her yourself this coming Thanksgiving. I expect you and Jackson here to come home to visit."

"I can't get the time off, but maybe you and Momma could come here instead."

Did she know what she was saying? Thanksgiving was weeks away. He might not ever be here on said holiday.

"I'll talk to her about it."

Jake swallowed another gulp of his coffee. What was Meghan going to do if they came for a visit and he no longer lived in Brooksville? That would destroy her story. Would her father force her to come home and marry that man she'd been promised to? The mere idea made his stomach ache.

No way could Jake play this marriage game forever,

though. She was just going to have to find another way to hold off her father. He couldn't be a part of it. He had a life in St. Louis, and he was going back to it hell or high water.

"Look at the time. I gotta go or I'll be late for work." She planted a kiss on Jake's cheek and went to place her dish in the sink. "Have a safe trip home, Daddy." She rubbed the man's shoulder and left the room.

Jake wished he was leaving too. But he was stuck here until Meghan returned since he didn't have his SUV. It was still sitting in front of the pharmacy.

****

"You sure you don't need me any longer?" Meghan asked Lyle, almost excited about getting home to Jackson. The night before had been more than she'd expected. She had never dreamed that copulation was for more than procreation. The church had taught her just the opposite. That's why it had never been high on her list of things to do. Yes, someday she wanted children, yet not until she was financially able, which was years from now.

"I'm good. You get on home. I'll see you in the morning."

She grabbed her purse and stepped out the back door, surprised to see Jackson leaning up against the front of his SUV.

"Hey. How'd you get into town?"

"I hitched a ride with your father. I wanted to save you another trip."

"That was thoughtful," she said, disappointed that he wouldn't be at home waiting for her.

"I need to get back to the compound. I didn't tell anyone I'd be gone for a few days. I'm going to have to lie the way it is. I need to keep you out of this. Both Andrew and Felix would be furious if they found out I was with you."

"I get it. Anyway, thanks again for helping me with Daddy. I refuse to go back to the life I had a year ago. So, I appreciate it."

He nodded. "I don't blame you one bit, Meghan. I better go, but I hope to see you soon."

Meghan held her breath as he got into his SUV. She watched as he backed out and took off. No hug or kiss goodbye. Not even a, 'I enjoyed our night together.' Though, she needed to remember, he'd had a sex life before her. Maybe their night of passion hadn't been all that exciting for him—a thought that clouded her eyes with unshed tears.

Enough, Meghan. It was only supposed to be one night. No repeat performances. Remember?

She rushed to her car and got in, angry with herself for her weakness. No man was worth crying over. She'd watched her momma do that too many times to count. God knows she didn't want that for herself. Besides, Jackson Gallagher belonged to a white supremacist group and that wasn't conducive to having a healthy relationship. She didn't care how amazing their night had been. He was more like her father and that was the last thing she wanted.

She started her car, determined to forget all about Jackson. Men like him were worthless in her eyes and she didn't need that in her life.

Instead of heading home, she'd go by her best friends Lily's, see if she'd wrapped the gifts they had bought for Violet. The shower was this weekend and the two were going to the event together.

She took a left off Main Street and drove another two blocks and turned right on to Everest. Lily lived in a small house, built in the early sixties—old but newer than the one Meghan lived in. Her friend worked as a beautician at the Cut & Curl, a shop that had three barber chairs, only two occupied now. So, Lily stayed busy since there were only four hair care shops in town, one of them inside the local retail store.

She pulled against the curb and killed the engine, intent on not saying a word about her and Jackson. Lily would only try to talk her into seeing him again, and that couldn't happen. Meghan wasn't going to let anyone sway her otherwise.

At the front door, she knocked and stood back, glancing around. Lily lived in a nice neighborhood. In the summers, they'd have block parties with barbeques and music, events she'd thoroughly enjoyed. Most of the people who lived there had children and they always had fun things to do for the kids. It was the perfect place to raise a family in Brooksville.

The door came open, and Lily's eyes widened. "Did we have plans?"

"Nope. I just thought I'd stop by to see if you are ready for the baby shower."

"More than ready. I'll show you how I wrapped everything up." She allowed Meghan inside and led her to the living room where the gifts sat on the floor wrapped. One of the boxes that held the outfits they'd bought was in a clear cellophane and had a pair of white, infant tennis shoes weaved through ribbon securing the top. "Oh My God, you are a genius. It looks amazing."

Lily blew on her fingers and rubbed on her chest. "I know, right. I should do this for a living."

"Yes, you should," Meghan agreed. "You have a gift. Just like with hair."

"If that's true, why haven't you even allowed me to cut yours?"

That was simple. Meghan could barely afford food, let alone something as frivolous as a thirty-dollar haircut. Hell, the money she'd spent on Jackson this morning was going to hurt at the end of the month.

"I don't have the time," she lied, not wanting to admit to her friend she was struggling.

"What are you doing right now? I have my shears. I can give you a cute bob that would look so good on you. I must admit that I've been wanted to get my hands on your hair since we first met."

"Why?"

"Because I think the longer hair doesn't do you justice."

Meghan was going to have to tell Lily the truth. "I really can't afford it. Thanks, though."

Her friend's eyes widened again. "I don't want any money, silly. We're best friends. Besides, you'd be a walking billboard for my talent. Come on. Please let me show you what I can do."

She stared at her friend, the excitement on her face more than what she could endure. "Okay. If you insist." Meghan had to admit she was looking forward to being pampered.

"Come on. Let's go to the kitchen. I have this new shampoo I wanted to try out anyway. You can be my first Guinee pig."

She followed her friend to the back of the house and wrapped a plastic cape around her neck, snapped it in place and brought her to the sink. Meghan had never had anyone wash her hair before and found it rather soothing, something she desperately needed right now.

Once the hair was clean, she toweled off the strands. "Sit down and I'll get started." Lily walked into her walk-in pantry a few feet away and returned with a black plastic roll with a tie holding it together. She quickly untied the string and rolled it out onto the table in front of Meghan. "Tools of the trade," her friend said, pulling out a pair of shears and a silver teethed comb.

Meghan squeezed her eyes closed as Lily started to cut, intent on not thinking about the strands of long hair she was removing. If she did, she might chicken out and stop her.

Maybe this was exactly what Meghan needed—a change that would not just alter her looks but her attitude. Perhaps Lyle's suggestion wouldn't seem all that crazy.

Hell, she'd never have to worry about paying the bills again. Strom's Pharmacy had been around for two generations and was successful. Meghan could keep it going since Lyle and his wife, who he lost fifteen years ago, never had any children. He wanted Meghan to take over and the only way for her to do that was to study Pharmacology. But years-worth of schooling? Could she afford the time and money? She wasn't sure. Not to mention, the closest college was miles and miles away. She had no idea how she could make it work. Maybe some on-line classes?

"I'm done," Lily said twenty-five minutes later, drawing Meghan back to the real world.

She opened her eyes as Lily pumped out some mouse and worked it through her tresses. "I bet you didn't realize that your hair has a natural curl now that it's jaw-length."

"Did you say jaw-length?" Meghan started to panic. Had her friend cut that much off?

"Yes. Wait until you see it before you freak out."

She grasped her shoulder and pulled her up. "Come and take a look in the bathroom."

Meghan allowed Lily to shove her along into the room, in front of the sink, her eyes widening at the image that met her. "What do you think?" her best friend asked, smiling next to her. Meghan continued to look at herself, unsure if it was even her staring back. This woman was stunning.

"You don't like it?"

Meghan shook her head, tears welling in her eyes.

"Oh, Meghan, I'm so sorry. I thought you'd like it."

"No, Lily. I love it. Is that really me?"

Her friend grinned. "Yes. It is. You look amazing. I told you, you would."

Meghan turned around and hugged her tight, overwhelmed by her new look. She never dreamed that a mere haircut could make her feel so different. "Thank you so much."

"You are more than welcome." She dragged her from the bathroom, back to the kitchen table. "Here. Take these products home to use. I have more at the shop."

"I don't know what to say, Lily."

"You don't have to say anything. After Violet's shower, I'm going to have more business than I can handle because you trusted me. You watch and see."

Chapter Eleven

On his hands and knees, Jake scrubbed the bathroom floor, wondering if this whole thing was worth it.

When he'd gotten back to the compound, he'd instantly been summoned to Andrew's office where he was interrogated about his whereabouts. He'd had to lie and say he'd met a lady at the local bar and had spent a few days in her bed. Not completely a lie. He and Meghan had spent a night together and he was still playing it over in his head, an event he was now paying for. He'd had to clean the whole compound from top to bottom to be able to stay. Almost a weeks' time cleaning and his palms were full of blisters to show for it all.

"Are you almost done in here?" Rim asked, standing over him. "I need to take a dump so you can clean the toilet again." What Jake wouldn't give to be able to slap that shit grin off his face. He loved every minute of Jake's humiliation. *Asshole.*

"I'll be done in a few minutes. Now, leave me alone."

"Fuck you." He turned on his heels and left, the irritating laughter while he did only making Jake angrier.

All the work had stalled him being able to learn anything about the crates of guns, though he knew they were no longer in the pantry since he'd had to clean that room too. The man had to have found a good hiding space. Jake had scrubbed every room in the place from top to bottom. They had to be somewhere else.

He finished the floor and rose, rubbing his lower back. Before leaving, he emptied the bucket into the sink and quickly rinsed it out. He was finished for the day. After returning the supplies to the back storage area, he headed for his room, running into Andrew on the way. *Shit.* Hopefully, he didn't have something else for him to do. Jake was exhausted.

"The place looks good, Jackson. You've done a fine job. In the morning, you can ride along with me to meet some of our acquaintances outside the compound. You need to get the feel of what we do here daily."

"Okay. Should I come by your office in the morning?"

"No. Just meet me out front at nine. We'll go from there."

"Will do. Night."

Andrew walked away.

Jake went to his room and closed the door. What did Andrew mean by him finding out what they did here? He had no idea, but maybe it'd help him with his story. That was his hope. Because he didn't want to spend any more time than he had to here with this bunch.

He eased down onto the bed, every bone in his body aching. He wasn't used to so much physical work.

As he was removing his boots, a knock at the door put him on alert. What now? Had Andrew changed his mind? Did he have something else for him to do?

He rose with some difficulty, padded across the room in his stocking feet and opened the door, finding Cullen.

"Can I come in?" he asked, glancing down the hall as if he was checking to see if anyone was watching.

"Sure." Jake stepped aside and allowed him in.

"Close the door."

Jake swallowed a lump of dread in his throat. Why would he want such privacy with him?

He did as instructed while turning to face the man. "What's going on?"

"I know that you lied to Andrew about where you were for those two days."

He was about to deny the fact when the man raised a hand to stop him. "I'm not going to tell him. You don't need to worry about that."

His words shocked Jake. Wasn't loyalty to Andrew paramount? "I don't get it. Why would you do that for me? I'm new here."

"I know who you are, Jake, and I believe I know why you're here."

He was screwed—his identity uncovered. But why tell him now. Why not just take him out somewhere and kill him?

"I'm going to trust you, Jake, with something that I probably shouldn't. But I'm here undercover with the ATF. I think you're here for a story. I don't want these two things to intersect. Do I make myself clear?"

"Okay. Yeah."

"When you were gone those two days, I was really hoping you'd come to your senses and left. It's dangerous to mess with these people if you don't know what you're doing. I came here tonight to try and talk you into leaving in the morning? Will you do that?"

Jake wished he could, but his career was everything to him and right now it was in tatters. "Look, I'm here for a reason. I need a story and until I have one, I'm staying. Maybe we could help one another. Do you know about those crates of guns that Felix Rim brought into the compound?"

"I didn't see the crates myself, but I did hear from my boys outside that they unloaded some last weekend. When Andrew was gone from the compound."

"Yeah, I was asked to put them into the pantry. They are no longer there. I overheard Rim saying he'd find another place to take them—that Andrew had no idea about the guns. Do you have any idea what they're planning?"

"No, but you can sure as hell bet I will. I gotta go. I still think you should leave. It's not safe for you."

"I'd imagine it's not all that safe for you, either. I can be here to watch your back and you can do the same for me, and maybe just maybe we can stop something bad from happening."

The man scowled at him but agreed. "If I can't get you to go, I'll keep my eyes peeled for trouble. Rim hates you. That's the guy you need to watch." He walked to the door and left.

Jake took in a ragged breath. He never would have thought that Cullen wasn't part of this hate group. The man could win an award for playing his part well. Jake had to make sure he didn't do anything to break his cover. This was way too important for the safety of the people here in town.

****

Meghan jumped into the passenger seat of Lily's car and closed the door.

"Are you excited about the shower?" her friend asked once she was buckled up. "Your hair looks great by the way."

"Thanks. I hope Violet likes what we got her."

"She will. Just try to relax and have fun. There are going to be some ladies there today you don't know. Some are nice, others not so much. I'll try to steer you are away from the latter."

Meghan leaned her head against the seat and took in a breath. "Thanks. I'm just lucky you and Violet come into the pharmacy, or I wouldn't have any friends."

Meghan was nervous about being around so many women. She'd learned, from her past, pending nuptials, that many single ladies could be petty, some downright resentful. Her ex-fiancé had been the catch of the county and he'd chosen her. She still didn't understand why, other than her daddy was the deacon at the church. Important, even when he was nothing more than an unemployed drunk.

"You okay?" Lily asked as she pulled up against the curb in front of Violet's mother's house.

"I'm fine." She opened the door. "Let's go have some fun."

The two grabbed the gifts from the trunk and headed for the front porch. Before they could knock, Violet rushed out, her face flushed with excitement. "Come in. You guys are the first to arrive."

Inside the house, Meghan glanced around, amazed at the size of Violet's mother's home, though her dad was a bank manager at Community Thrust, the largest branch in the region. Every piece of furniture was quality and gleamed, her mother knowing how to keep a house.

"Go ahead and place the gifts on the small table next to the wall and go get something to eat. I tried the punch. It's good." She rubbed her big belly. "Everyone else should be showing up any minute now."

Meghan placed her basket down and headed for the

food table. She grabbed a plate, filled it, poured a cup of punch and went to sit at one of the six folding tables in the room. Lily joined her and ate as women started filing into the room, all looking at both her and Lily who they smiled at. Meghan couldn't blame them for not giving her the same attention—she was a stranger. Unless they recognized her from the pharmacy.

Soon, all the tables were filled, and everyone was chatting. A young woman, in her late teens, leaned over to Meghan. "I love your hair. Did Lily cut it?"

"Yes, on Tuesday."

"It really looks great."

Lily smiled at her from across the table.

"I'm Violet's sister. You must be Meghan. You work at Strom's pharmacy, right?"

"I do, yes."

"I'm getting ready to go to college spring semester. I'm so excited about that."

"Really? Where are you going?"

"Maryville College in St. Louis."

"How does your mom feel about that?"

"She wants me to get the best education I can. I got a full academic scholarship. I was lucky."

Wow. She really was. Not that her parents probably couldn't afford the cost. Meghan would have to get some kind of Pell grant to go since she didn't have any money saved.

Another red-haired woman stepped up to their table. "I love your hair," the lady said. "Where'd you get it cut?" She touched a strand of Meghan's hair, rubbing it between her fingers. "Nice."

"You know full well who cut her hair, Wendy, and, no, you can't poach her from me."

"I wasn't going to do that. What product did you use on her?"

"Like I'd tell you."

The woman huffed and walked away.

"I didn't realize how competitive beauticians were."

Lily grimaced. "You don't know the half of it. Wendy has taken three of my steady clients in the past year. I'm not letting that happen again. That woman is a viper."

"I've never seen her. She doesn't come into Strom's."

"She wouldn't since she works inside our local department store. They have a pharmacy."

"Okay, ladies, let's open presents. My daughter refuses to wait until after the baby games."

Violet joined them at their table and was handed one gift after another, the oohs and aahs echoing through the house for the next twenty-five minutes. After the gift opening, the games began, and Meghan played along, never having had so much fun.

The last of the games were written questions that they were supposed to guess about Violet's pregnancy. *What was the first symptom you had? Did you have morning sickness? How long did it last? Did you have any strange cravings? Was it something that you liked before you were pregnant?*

Meghan had no idea. She'd never known anyone who was pregnant personally until now and she'd never asked her anything about the experience. She'd have to guess at them all.

Once everyone placed their pencils down, Violet's mother stood up and repeated the questions. "First symptom," Violet said. "My breasts started to hurt."

Meghan frowned at Lily who returned the gesture.

"Yes, I did have morning sickness, but it was at night, and it lasted until the end of my fourth month."

"That long?" Meghan asked.

"Yep. Not a pretty picture for sure."

"Cravings. It wasn't anything too weird. But I couldn't get enough cream soda. Seemed to be the only thing that'd calm my stomach. I drank it occasionally before I was pregnant but not like now."

Meghan got zero right. She was bad at this game thing. But it was entertaining, nonetheless.

An hour later, she and Lily, after helping clean up, left the house. On Main Street, she caught sight of Jackson's SUV parked at Culverts. He and Andrew were sitting outside talking to someone she didn't recognize. Seeing him again sent her heart fluttering.

Dang it. Why couldn't she forget about him? Get on with her life like before they'd met?

"Let's stop and get some ice cream," Lily said, putting on her blinker to turn.

"Do we have to? I have things to do at home." It was a lie, but she couldn't face Jackson right now. She wasn't ready.

"We'll get it to go. It'll only take a few minutes."

This was the last thing Meghan wanted but what could she say? Not the truth. Maybe he wouldn't even notice her, and she could get in and out without even a backwards glance.

She exited the car, thankful the outdoor seating was on the driver's side of the car and the front entrance was directly ahead of her.

Meghan made a beeline for the door, walked up to the counter and ordered a sweet tea, not at all hungry for ice cream. She was too nervous for that.

"That's all your getting?" Lily's cornflower blue eyes narrowed.

"Yeah, I'm still full from the shower."

"Come on. You barely ate anything."

Lily ordered a vanilla cone and the two started for the door, only to be bombarded by Jackson coming inside. She was stuck. There was no other way out. She tried to hide behind her friend but when he entered the building, Jackson saw her, and his eyes widened. He looked almost as nervous as she felt. Still, it'd been over a week since she'd seen him. He seemed to be avoiding her as well. Suddenly, she wondered why.

"Ladies," he said once they were side by side.

"Hello. We were just leaving." Meghan grabbed her friend's arm and tugged her toward the exit. She was getting out of there before Jackson had a chance to say another word. Hearing his deep baritone might change her mind about not having anything to do with him again. She could still hear his whispers against her ear.

Outside, Meghan released a breath and got in the car, squeezing her eyes closed, trying to calm her racing heart.

"Are you okay?"

She glanced at her friend and nodded. "You know how I feel about that hate group. I just don't want to be around them."

"I know but you didn't have to run a marathon to get away. I couldn't keep up," she said, grinning at her.

Lily started the car and was pulling away when Meghan remembered the other man Jackson and Andrew were sitting with. "Do you know who that guy in the leather jacket is who's sitting at the table with Andrew

Gibson?" It didn't really matter. Meghan was just curious because she'd never seen him before.

"He looks familiar, but I can't be sure."

Meghan stared at the man, making a mental note of his features. Monday, if she remembered to do so, she'd ask Lyle. If the man lived in Brooksville, he'd know who he was and where the man resided since he'd lived here all his life.

Chapter Twelve

Jake lay in bed, wondering why Meghan wouldn't even talk to him at Culver's. Maybe she was angry because he hadn't seen her since the day her father left. He should have told her he'd be busy for a few days— getting back in the swing of things here at the compound. Hell, he'd almost been kicked out and had spent day and night paying for those two nights with her. Of course, he couldn't tell her that. She'd raced off before he had a chance.

He still didn't understand why Andrew had wanted him to meet Trent Hammon today, a corn and soybean farmer who lived seven miles east of town. The guy and Andrew talked pleasantries, nothing that Jake would've needed to be there for. The whole thing was strange. But he was sure there was a reason behind it that he simply hadn't figured out yet.

He rose and reached for the notebook under the dresser and wrote down all he'd learned, no matter how insignificant it seemed. Afterwards, he tucked the pad back in his hiding place. As he did, his stomach started to gnaw at his backbone. He hadn't eaten since breakfast.

He and Andrew had met Hammon at the ice cream parlor around two but hadn't gotten food and when they got back supper was already put away.

Jake would run down to the kitchen and make a sandwich.

When he started down the second hallway, voices from Andrew's office stopped him in his tracks. He inched closer to the door. One of the voices was Andrews; the other, he didn't recognize. "Can he get us what we need?" the other man asked.

"Yeah, but it's going to take a few weeks. He doesn't want to get flagged by authorities."

"That's going to slow down our timeline."

"I'm okay with that since we don't want to rush this and make any mistakes. If Hammon needs the time, I'm going to give him that," Andrew said.

Jake had no idea when Andrew and Trent had this conversation. It wasn't while he was with the two.

Wait. He had gone inside to use the restroom for a few minutes. When he'd run into Meghan. Maybe that's when the two had talked.

What was going to take weeks to get? Jake had no idea, but he had a foreboding feeling about it. Maybe this was something he should tell Cullen. Maybe he'd know what they were discussing. Jake certainly didn't. He still couldn't believe the man was working undercover for ATF. Jake would never have guessed since he certainly fit in looks-wise with the group.

"Okay, keep me posted," the other guy said, sounding as if he had moved closer to the door.

Jake had better get out of there before he got caught. He shot around the corner and headed for the kitchen, replaying the conversation over in his head. The more he did, the more ominous the whole thing became. Andrew was planning something. He needed to find out what. But how? Who was the guy Andrew was talking to? If he knew that, it might help him figure out what the two were up to. He also needed to learn how that Kennett character played into all of this. Why had the man disappeared? Maybe the local library's archives would have something on him? Come morning, he'd break away from the compound and do some digging.

In the kitchen, he was relieved to find it empty. He walked to the refrigerator, opened the double doors and looked inside. Everything he needed to make a sandwich was on the middle shelf.

He quickly slapped some turkey and cheese between two slices of bread, wrapped it in a napkin and started back toward the door, thinking it best to avoid anyone else that evening. Jake would still love to get even with Rim for the headache he'd given him but that'd only get him kicked to the curb.

At the door, he heard another set of voices, one Rim's, the other was the guy he was with the night Jake learned about those gun crates. He still had no idea who he was. So much for getting to know everyone there.

Dammit all to hell. How was he going to avoid Rim? He could hide in the pantry and hope they didn't come inside. *No.* That'd just be stupid. He needed to stand his ground with a man like him. That was the only way to get him to leave him alone.

He took a breath and stepped out the door, not bothering to acknowledge Rim's presence. Jake simply walked past him, like he hadn't a care in the world.

"Fuck you, Gallagher," Felix said as he passed.

Jake didn't bother to respond. He was just trying to goad him into a fight and Jake didn't give two shits what the man thought of him. He was a nobody. A disgusting Nazi and all Jake wanted to do was go back to his room and eat his sandwich in peace.

"You ain't got nothing to say, sissy boy?"

Jake clenched his empty fist, an urge to use it on the man's face becoming all-consuming.

He turned back. "You're going to get yourself knocked out if you don't shut your trap, Felix. I can only take so much."

The man cackled. "I'm shaking in my boots. Who got the jump on who last time?"

"You hit me from behind, asshole. You think that's getting the jump on me? That's a cheap shot from an insecure, little man."

Rim's eyes widened and he stepped back, why Jake didn't realize until he heard Andrew's voice over his shoulder. "What's this about hitting Jackson from behind, Felix? When did this happen?"

Silence filled the hallway. The only thing heard was heavy breathing. Not Jake's. But Rim's.

"Well?" Andrew prompted, staring Felix down.

"All right. All right." Felix shook his head. "I wacked him with a pitcher the day he disappeared. No big deal. He walks around like he's God's gift and I'd had enough. Okay?"

Andrew's eyes narrowed to slits, his mouth thinning into a fine line.

Jake didn't want to stir Rim up any more than he already had. "It's okay, Andrew. I got over it. Just had a headache for a few days. That's all."

"That doesn't matter. In my house, there's no retribution unless I okay it. Did I give that to you, Felix?"

"No, boss. I'm sorry. I was still angry about Meghan. Every time I look at Gallagher, I think of her."

Jake sneered. The man was a disgusting pig. How had he survived this long without someone taking his ass out?

"Get out of my sight, Felix. I'll decide what I'm going to do with you in the morning."

"Yes, sir." Felix bolted down the hall and disappeared around the corner.

The man he'd been talking to just stood there, looking amused. "You got something to say, Bart?" Andrew asked the guy Jake had never met.

"Nope. See you in the morning."

When he'd gone, Andrew turned his attention to Jake. "Why didn't you tell me about Felix's attack?"

"I can take care of myself. I'm not about to tattle on some guy who has emotional issues. It would just make things worse."

"You're right." Andrew nodded. "I'll see you tomorrow."

Jake headed for his room, intent on keeping his eyes peeled for Rim. If he had to wager a bet, the man was even angrier than before, which put Jake in an even more precarious situation. He'd need to watch his back, or he just might end up with a knife stuck in it.

****

Meghan rose from bed, feeling like she was going to throw up. She quickly slapped a cold rag behind her neck and checked the time on the wall clock. 3:30 in the morning. Boy, was it going to be a long day, especially if she felt like this at work.

Why was she so nauseous? It wasn't flu season. No one she knew had been sick. Maybe it'd been something she ate. That was probably it.

She left the bathroom and walked to the kitchen to get something to help her feel better. A couple of antacids might do the trick.

While popping two in her mouth, she glanced out

the window, the moon above full and bright. It lit up the whole backyard. When she was about to head back to her bedroom, a glow of something red from next to a tree had her straining her eyes to make out what it was. A figure leaned against a large Maple next to the fence-line, smoking a cigarette.

Meghan's heart started to pound. This time it couldn't be her father. He didn't smoke. Jackson didn't either. The only person she knew who did was Rim. But would the guy defy his boss? Going against his demand to stay away from her?

She rushed to check the doors to make sure they were secure and raced back to the kitchen. Meghan was glad she hadn't turned on any lights when she came to get the pills. At least he hadn't seen her looking out the window. He had no idea she knew he was there.

Should she call the police? Last time she did, that didn't go so well. Maybe Jackson would come and help. Too bad she didn't have his phone number.

Meghan glanced back out the window. The shadow was still there, though he'd finished his cigarette. If indeed it was Felix, what was he planning? To break in?

The thought brought another wave of nausea to her stomach and acid working its way up her throat. All she needed was to have to go throw up right now. Perhaps Lyle was right. It really wasn't wise to live this far out of town. Being single with no protection. As soon as possible, she'd start searching for another place to stay. This was getting too risky for her. Right now, though, that wasn't going to help.

She snuck to her bedroom and found the bat propped next to the head of her bed, grabbed the handle and her cell phone, walking back to the kitchen. Until morning, she was going to have to watch and see if the guy moved. If he inched any closer to the house, she'd call 9-1-1. The deputy might be able to catch the stalker this time, if he got the jump on him.

Wait. What if the first time hadn't been her father? Why hadn't she asked him if he'd been out here the night before? That would have been the smart thing to do. Too bad she'd been so shocked to see him that she hadn't thought about it. It was more likely to have been someone else since her father had a back problem and two bad knees. He probably couldn't outrun a toddler. And now that she thought about it, the first guy had been taller than both Rim and her dad.

That realization brought on more anxiety. Who'd been watching her and why?

Meghan sucked in a ragged breath and stared at the shadow, straining her eyes to get a better look at his face. Unfortunately, he was too far away, and half shaded by the tree branches.

She clutched the bat, twisting her hand around the base, anxious and apprehensive. What would happen if she turned on a light? Would he leave or try to break in? Meghan wished she knew what to do.

Her mouth went dry, and she swallowed, choking on the saliva as it forced its way down her tight throat.

She had to do something before she died of fright. But what?

Meghan had friends she could call but that would be putting them at risk. She couldn't do that. She loved them too much.

Just call the police. She had the deputy's card. Where had she placed it? Her mind raced, trying to remember. Movement from the tree kicked up her heartrate.

She watched, her fingers wrapping tightly around the handle of the bat. Meghan wasn't going to go out without a fight.

She held her breath until the figure moved through the gate and disappeared. He might be gone but that didn't mean he wouldn't come back. She needed to pack a bag and get out of there. She could stay with Lily for a few days while she looked for another place to live. Someone was obsessed with her, and it wasn't safe to be alone. Not anymore. Especially this far from town.

Chapter Thirteen

Jake finished loading the dishwasher and turned the twitch to wash. Now, he'd go back to his room and change. He had about four hours to get to the library and get some info on that missing man since he'd need to be back before lunchtime.

In his room, he quickly changed into clean clothes, tucked some paper from his notebook inside his jacket pocket and left again, heading for the front door. He'd about made it out when Andrew's voice from behind stopped him. Jake turned around.

"I'm glad I caught you. I need you to do me a favor."

"What's that?"

Andrew met him at the door and held out a slip of paper. "I need you to get this for me."

Jake glanced at the note that had pseudoephedrine written on it. *Shit.* Was he making Meth now. Was this a bad episode of *Breaking Bad.*

To top it off, he'd have to go to Strom's to pick it up, and Jake could already see the look of incrimination on that beautiful face of Meghan's.

"Okay. I'll see you later." Andrew turned and headed for his office.

Jake blew out a breath as he left the compound. He did have to admit that seeing Meghan again after two and a half weeks brought a tingle of excitement to his extremities. Even if she didn't feel the same about him.

The night they spent together had been amazing, even though he hadn't been thrilled about taking her virginity. Surprisingly though, she'd been an avid student—learned right away how to respond. He missed her. Maybe this trip could work to his advantage. Perhaps he could get things straightened out with her so they could spend more time together.

Ten minutes later had him sitting in front of the pharmacy, reevaluating what he'd been thinking about. What if she was still angry? She had this if-looks-could-kill-expression. If he saw that, he'd back off and try another tact.

He popped the door and jumped out of his SUV, thoughts running amok in his head. Inside, he glanced around. *Just stay focused. The worst that could happen is she'll tell you to leave.*

Jake walked to the back counter, spotting the old man who suggested he and Meghan spend those nights together. Maybe he should thank him for that. Or perhaps he shouldn't since now he was fixated on her instead of getting his career back on track.

"Jackson," the man said, seemingly happy to see him. "What brings you in?"

"I need to get some pseudoephedrine for a friend."

The older man stared at him intently. "This could take a few minutes. I think we got a new shipment in but haven't had time to get to it yet," he said in a tone that suggested he was no longer thrilled he'd come in.

"How about I drop by later to pick it up. Would that be all right?" Jake didn't see Meghan. There was no need to stick around. He could get the medicine after his visit to the library.

The older man headed for the back room.

Jake left the pharmacy, got back into his vehicle and headed for the library. Outside the building he spotted Meghan's friend that she was with at Culver's.

He met her at the door and opened it for her and followed her inside. "Thank," she said and gave him a warm smile. "You're welcome. Tell Meghan I said hello."

Her eyes widened. "You know Meghan?"

Jake was a little surprised her friend didn't know about him. He thought women talked about everything. Still, maybe she was embarrassed about what happened between them, especially since she thought he was one of the BWN group. That could be why her friend hadn't been told.

"Meghan helped me out when I had a hard hit to my noggin. She's a very kind person."

"Yes, she is. Funny though, she didn't say anything about that."

"How's she doing?"

"She's staying with me right now. Someone was sneaking around her place. It's not safe for her to stay that far out of town anymore."

"And she's sure it wasn't her father again?"

"Her father?" the brunette asked, her eyes widening.

Why kind of friends were these two? Apparently, Meghan didn't tell her anything.

"Maybe you should ask her. I gotta do some research right now. Like I said, ask Meghan about it."

Jake strode toward the back, found the archive area, and sat down. He typed in Kennett's name. The headline that came up said **MISSING LOCAL MAN**. He skimmed the article and found out that he'd been missing for a year. He was a local, worked at the municipal building in Planning and Zoning. A single guy. No children. Could have been missing longer because of that. Not even the people he'd worked with noticed he was missing until the police got involved. Talk about a painful realization. That no one cared to acknowledge his absence. That was one thing Jake didn't want.

Maybe a consuming career wasn't all that it was cracked up to be? That having someone to love and to be loved by was more important.

Jake shook the thought and jotted down all the information he could gel from the next three stories pertaining to the man, who to this day, didn't seem to be missed by anyone.

He folded the legal pad paper and rose, then headed for the exit. Now that he'd done the research, his thoughts traveled back to Meghan. Who was watching her? Was it Felix? He wouldn't put it past the guy. Andrew was blind to assume that Rim would obey him. Look at what Felix said about those crates of guns. He didn't give two shits about defying his boss. The man was all about himself. Jake wouldn't even be surprised if he tried to overthrow Andrew, that a Coup was in the works. But should Jake voice his concerns? Did he really care if Andrew and his Nazi group killed each other? Not really. The world would be a much better place without them.

He left the library and started back toward the pharmacy. Meghan was safe for now. Being in town helped a lot and she had her friend to protect her. He wouldn't need to worry. She might not care about what happened to him, but he cared about her. Like it or not.

****

Meghan stepped around the counter, toting a box of

cold medicine she had to shelf. She also had discount tags to put beneath the ones on sale. Her nerves were on edge every time the door signaled someone was coming in. Lyle had told her Jackson had come to pick up, of all things, pseudoephedrine. What the hell did he need that for? Did he have a cold or was it for something much more nefarious? She really couldn't picture that.

She shook the thought and went to work, placing all the medicine and their pricing in the medicine aisle. When she'd finished, she took the tape off the box and folded it. On the way back to the counter, Meghan's stomach started to churn again. She was getting tired of this nausea. She'd had it all morning, spent most of her time in the bathroom. She had no idea what had caused it since she hadn't eaten anything out of the ordinary. But something was making her sick.

Behind her, the door chimed, causing her heartrate to pick up pace. She turned and that same speeding heart skipped a beat. Why did this happen every time she saw him. He wasn't worthy of the reaction.

He reached her and smiled, only causing her head to swim, to the point that she felt faint.

She grasped his forearm when her knees wobbled.

Before she went down, he scooped her up into his arms, his amazing blue eyes widening. "Are you okay?" he asked glancing around the room. "Where's Lyle?"

"He's in the back. I'm fine. Just weak from food poisoning. You can put me down now."

"How's you get food poisoning?"

"I don't know if it's that or not. It could be a stomach bug."

He frowned. "Maybe you should see a doctor? Find out for sure?"

"If it's not gone by tomorrow, I will." She struggled to get him to release her.

He set her onto her feet yet held her arm, unsure if she was steady enough to let go.

"I'm okay, Jackson. Don't you have some place to be?" His hovering was wreaking havoc on her nerves—his scent alone making her heartrate pitch. The man was like kryptonite, made her knees weak.

He finally released her and stepped back.

Thank the Lord. She could breathe again.

"I heard you are staying in town with your friend. What happened last night to bring that about?"

"Someone was sneaking around again, and it wasn't Daddy. This guy was a smoker. The only man I know who smokes is Felix. Though, I don't think it was him either. This dude was tall, like the first intruder. I got to thinking about that first time. Daddy would never have been able to outrun the officer that night. He has a back injury and bad knees."

"Any idea who it could have been? Anyone besides Felix who has an interest in you that you can think of? Someone who comes in here a lot, maybe?"

Meghan thought about the question and came up short. "Nobody I can think of offhand, no."

"Maybe spend some time going over that in your head. You might surprise yourself."

"Okay. I will. Thanks. I have to get back to work." This discussion was not helping her. It was time to put an end to it.

"Right. I do too." He looked as if he wanted to say something else, but she refused to let him.

She turned and headed to the back room. Lyle could deal with him and his pseudoephedrine purchase.

Meghan needed distance. He caused strange feelings inside her, and she didn't like that.

She inhaled a deep breath, catching a hint of his scent on the sleeve of her shirt. *Just great.* Now she was going to smell like him all day and that was going to drive her crazy. This whole thing was stupid. Just because she slept with Jackson didn't mean she'd lost all control of her faculties. That had always been a virtue of hers, a strength, and she refused to allow *a man* to change that about herself. Especially a hate monger.

With that in mind, she focused on work. She found another box that had been delivered that morning and used her knife to cut open the top, finding pregnancy tests inside. Seeing them brought back the odd symptoms she'd been having.

When was her last period? Why couldn't she remember. It had only been a few weeks. Could she even have symptoms this soon?

She swallowed hard as she stared at the tests. What if she was pregnant? What would she do?

Hadn't Jackson used a condom? Oh, God. Could one have broken?

She grabbed one of the test kits from the box and flipped it over, reading the instructions on the back.

Should she or shouldn't she?

Did she really want to know right now? Maybe she should wait a few more days. But if she did that, she'd be in agony not knowing.

Chapter Fourteen

Jake placed the notes he'd formulated earlier inside the journal under his dresser, feeling tired yet anxious. Seeing Meghan earlier that day, her face pale and gaunt troubled him. For whatever reason, he wished he was with her now instead of here, alone, worrying about her welfare.

A tap at the door and it opening, had him bolting upright and tucking his book under his pillow.

He was relieved to see it was Cullen.

"Can I come in?" His deep frown line on his forehead gave Jake pause.

He waved him inside and stood. "What's going on?"

"Something big is about to happen. Andrew has something brewing with Hammon and Dean Cambridge, the Farmers Insurance guy here in town."

"Any idea what?" Jake tried to connect the two men and what Andrew would have going on with them.

"I don't and suddenly he's not talking to me. I hope my cover hasn't been blown."

Jake's stomach made a nosedive. That was his worst nightmare. For Andrew to find out why he was here. "How would he have been able to do that? Any clue? You've been here a while now, right."

"Almost a year. Right after he bought this compound."

"Were you here when Kennett disappeared?"

"That's why I was sent in. To try and find out what happened to the guy. Rumors were swirling that Andrew had him killed. No real clue as to why either."

"Did he know something he shouldn't have, or was it for personal reasons?"

"I think he found out something that Andrew didn't want to come out. He made sure it didn't."

"Did you hear anything that could give us a clue where the guy was killed, who might have done it? Seems to me that Andrew doesn't do any dirty work himself. He has others do it for him."

Cullen shook his head. "No. No one has slipped up and said a thing but people in town are still talking about it. Sheriff Hanson and his deputies are watching Andrew. For Andrew to be planning something with all that attention, is just arrogant."

"We need to find out what he's up to. Maybe the sheriff could talk to this Dean character. Lean on him a little bit. I could go and talk to him."

"That's an idea. I'm afraid if I go, Andrew might hear about it. You're new. No one knows you yet. It might go unnoticed, especially since you've come and gone before."

"I'll talk to him in the morning. That's if Andrew doesn't have plans for me."

"I better get out of here. Keep your eyes and ears open. This could mean life or death for someone." Cullen slipped out the door, leaving Jake to wonder what Andrew was planning. He didn't come across as a cold-blooded killer. Though, did anyone, really?

He reached under his pillow and jotted down what Cullen had just told him and tucked the notebook back under his dresser.

On his bed, he breathed in some air and looked up at the ceiling. So many things to think about. So much to be concerned with. Between Andrew and Meghan, he'd be lucky to get any sleep. Nothing new. Ever since he'd arrived in Brooksville, he'd barely gotten any rest, besides that first night at Meghan's house. He'd give about anything to be there right now. With her. Preferably alone. In her bed and wrapped in her arms.

Now, he was never going to get any sleep. Why bother even trying?

He swung his legs over the side of the bed, grabbed his boots and pulled them on. He snatched his wallet from the night table and left the room. He was going to find an all-night diner and get some coffee, think about what he'd say to the sheriff when he saw him. As quietly as he could, he made his way down the hallway and left through the front door, making sure it was locked. In his SUV, he inhaled a deep breath, feeling somehow lighter being on the other side of the compound. The place sucked the life right out of him. He didn't belong with those people. He was much happier with Meghan.

He drove through town, dim lights illuminating all the storefronts. At the other end of town was a gas station/ diner. He parked off to the side and headed into the café. Once inside, he found a booth in the back where no one that drove by could see him. Andrew had too many spies. He didn't need someone ratting on him.

A middle-aged woman in a bright pink shirt and a pair of black slacks headed his way, grabbing for a pad and pen tucked in a white apron around her waist.

"Hello. What can I get you tonight?"

"Just coffee for now, thanks."

"Coming right up."

Jake leaned back and played with the paper napkin that was wrapped around the silverware on the table. A ticking in the background had to be from a clock somewhere in the room. He glanced around and found it right behind the counter where the cash register sat. It was 2:30 in the morning. He had hours before he could go to the sheriff's office.

The waitress returned with a large mug and filled it to the brim with coffee, the smell instantly reviving him.

"Thank you." He gave her a smile.

"If you need anything else, let me know." She walked back behind the counter.

He took a sip of the coffee, noting it wasn't all that bad for this time of night. Most places it would have been stout and bitter. This was neither.

The door chiming brought his attention to the door where he saw a tall, blond-haired man stepping inside and going to sit at the counter where there were ten rounded stools, bright red in color, matching the rest of the café's retro deco, including the booth seats. There was something eerie about the guy, but Jake couldn't put a finger on what.

The man order coffee as well and had his attention glued to his phone. Typical. Jake would have been doing the same if he had his. What else was there to do.

The mirror that covered the wall behind the counter gave Jake the opportunity to study the guy's face. Handsome in a way. Maybe close to forty. He was dressed nice. Was he from town or just passing through. The journalist in him had his mind spinning with all kinds of questions.

The man looked up, caught Jake staring at him in the mirror and spun on his stool, picking up his coffee and heading toward him.

"Can I join you?" He studied Jake was an intensity that was unnerving.

What could he say? No? "Sure."

"What brings you in here so late tonight?" he asked Jake.

"I was going to ask you the same question."

"I'm just heading out of town and thought coffee could help keep me awake." He lounged back in the booth, draping his arm on the back of the seat. He seemed to be in no hurry to get going. "What about you?"

"I couldn't sleep."

He pointed to Jake's cup. "And you thought coffee would help."

Jake laughed. "Definitely not conducive to sleeping, true. So, what brought you to Brooksville?"

The man grinned. "Why don't you see if you can guess."

Jake examined him for a moment. "It's either work or a woman. You don't really look like you're dressed for a business thing. I'd say a woman."

The man nodded. "Very good deduction. You're not a detective, are you?"

"Nope. Just an observer. So, tell me about this woman you came to town to see?"

The question seemed to make the man tense up. "She's actually an ex but I came to see if we couldn't reconnect."

"You don't say? I've never felt a need to go back and reminisce, myself. She must have been something special."

He shrugged. "I guess. Well, I better get a move on. I got a long drive ahead of me. Nice meeting you."

"You too. Have a safe trip home."

The man rose and stopped at the counter to pay for his coffee and left the café. As he headed for his car, he lit up a cigarette. A lot of people smoked. Too many. Rim reeked of the crap all the time.

Jake shook the thought and took a long drink of his cooling coffee. This day had dragged on and it wasn't even close to daylight yet.

****

Meghan stared at the stick in her hand, too shocked to move. How could this possibly be happening to her? The one and only time she had sex, with protection no less, and she found herself in this mess. She could go back to her roots and say it was God's will, but she didn't believe that, not any longer. This was bad luck.

What was she going to do? Could it be a false positive? Should she take another test?

She shook her head, swallowing a mouthful of acid that rose in her throat. She ran the water over a washcloth and slapped it behind her neck. That always worked to calm her stomach. She had to get going or she was going to be late for work.

On the way to the door, she ran into Lily, who smiled. When she noticed the cloth, she frowned. "Are you okay?"

"Stomach's just a little queasy. I'll be fine."

"Are you sure?"

Meghan nodded. "Yep. I got to run. See you after work."

In the car, she flipped the cloth over and pulled away from the curb. Once she was at work, she'd find something safe to take for her nausea and get on with the day. Her situation couldn't affect her job performance. It was even more important to keep it now.

She took the turn into the back-alley parking area of Strom's and cut the engine. On the dash, the clock flashed ten till eight. Only a few minutes to get her stuff put away, while praying her stomach didn't revolt.

As she was headed for the front counter, she ran into Lyle and smiled. "Good morning."

He stared at her for what seemed like forever, making her feel uncomfortable.

"You got something to tell me?" he asked.

"What do you mean?"

"You know I've been a pharmacist for fifty years, missy, and have seen my share of expectant women in that time. You got the look."

Meghan's jaw dropped. How could he possibly know that from her appearance? Did she have pregnant stamped on her forehead? No way could she lie and deny the truth. The man was like a grandfather—closer to her than her own father.

He turned, walked down an aisle, and returned a few moments later and handed her a box. "That should help with the nausea and safe to take in your condition." He handed her a bottle. "Take one of those a day. Pregnant women need vitamins. It might help you feel less tired cause you look all washed-out. Have you been eating okay?"

"Yes, I have, but you're not going to lecture me on the sin of premarital sex, and how at my age, I should have known better?"

He adjusted the glasses on the tip of his nose and huffed. "You know I'm no holy roller, and I'm sure you are already scolding yourself about this. Why kick the dead rabbit?"

She couldn't have loved this man any more than she did at that moment. He knew she was damning herself. She didn't need him to add to her misery.

"I appreciate that."

"Go take one of the anti-nausea pills now, and later, when you start feeling better, you can take the other."

Meghan rushed to do what her boss asked. She returned as the doorbell chimed a person's entrance. She craned her head to see who came in, but Lyle stood in the way. "Is Meghan around?" a voice asked, and her stomach lurched into her throat.

Jackson. She couldn't let him see her like this. Not when Lyle had known of her condition just by looking at her. Though, he was accustomed to seeing pregnant women. She was sure Jackson wasn't.

"Yep. She is. What do you want with her?" Lyle asked in a tone Meghan had never heard him use before.

He knew Jackson was the reason she was in trouble. Yet, Meghan couldn't blame Jackson for this. She had begged him to take her virginity. He had no culpability here. This was all her fault.

"She wasn't feeling well the other day when I came in. I wanted to stop in to check on her."

"She's doing fine. You don't need to worry. Why don't you go on now? We all have work to get to."

Lyle was protecting her. Maybe he too was concerned that Jackson would figure out what was happening with her, and he hadn't had a chance to talk to her about her plans. If she was going to keep the baby or not. She appreciated that.

"Okay. Tell her I stopped by."

"I will."

Meghan held her breath until the door chimed, and

she blew out the strangled breath. She wasn't even sure if she was going to tell him yet and she was grateful for the reprieve. The next time she saw him though, she'd have a decision to make. To tell him, or not.

Chapter Fifteen

Jake entered the police station, still not sure what he was going to say to the sheriff. He reached the front desk and smiled at the petite woman in a dark uniform sitting behind the glass partition.

She returned the gesture and asked, "What can I do for you today?"

"I'd like to speak to the sheriff if he has time."

"Can I tell him what it's pertaining to?"

"It's about a missing local. I'd like to ask him a few questions."

She rose. "Go ahead and take a seat. I'll see if he's free."

Jake walked to the waiting area and sat on the chair adjacent to a large picture window and watched the traffic go by, his encounter with Lyle Strom in the forefront of his mind. He seemed annoyed with Jake. Was it because of his past visit and the pseudoephedrine thing or was it something else? He couldn't be sure.

He'd really wanted to see Meghan. He was worried about her. The last time he'd run into her she didn't look well. Was stress getting to her? Why did he care? She didn't seem to acknowledge him after what they'd shared—treated him like a pariah, and to say that bothered him was an understatement. It pissed him off. Still, he might have done that when he knew the relationship wouldn't go anywhere. A couple of times that he could think of, off hand. Maybe he deserved what Meghan was dishing out.

"The sheriff will see you now," the officer said, startling him back to the present.

Jake rose and followed her down the hall to the last room on the right. The man sitting behind the desk was athletic looking in the same black uniform, his head bald and shiny. Typical bad cop look. Suddenly, he wasn't sure about talking to him. He'd seen this before. Law enforcement resembling White Supremacists. A lot of that crew had infiltrated the force, and this man certainly looked the part. Maybe he and Andrew were friends, and if that was the case, it'd get back to him that Jake came by. *Shit.* Now what was he going to do?

"Go ahead and take a seat, Mr…?" Maybe he should use his real name. Perhaps he could avoid this getting into the hands of the wrong people. Though, doing so, could blow his cover right out of the water.

What the hell should he do? Best to use his real name since the sheriff could do a background check on him after he left.

"Jake Mills. I'm a freelance reporter and I'm doing a follow-up story on one of your missing residents."

The sheriff's hazel eyes narrowed. "Who is that?"

"Steven Kennett. I believe he's been missing a year now."

"Yes, but we also have something tentative about the man traveling to Canada to stay with family. We're still waiting for confirmation on that."

Seemed pretty sketchy to Jake. Was the sheriff even telling the truth?

"When do you plan to hear something?" he asked, watching the man's reactions. Jake had always been good at reading people. Hopefully, he could in this case.

"Within a few weeks," the sheriff said, his eyes connecting with his. Nothing. Not even a flinch. Maybe he was telling the truth. This Kennett disappearance could all be just a man picking up and leaving town.

"So, what you are telling me is there is no story there?"

"More of a misunderstanding, I would say. But until it's confirmed, he's still a missing person. May I ask why him? There must be hundreds of missing person cases. Why choose Steven Kennett? Even when he lived here, no one noticed him. It took days for anyone to realize he was gone."

"Exactly. Why not him? He apparently had a family in Canada. So many people slip through the cracks of our system. That was the angle I was aiming for." Damned if he wasn't getting awful good at lying—to a law enforcement office at that.

"Sorry I couldn't be more help. If you give me your card, I can call you when I hear something."

Shit. Jake never expected him to contact him. He couldn't allow that. "That's all right. I'll check back in a few weeks. Thanks for your time, Sheriff."

He rose and left the man's office. Jake could only imagine what he was thinking about his impromptu visit. Hopefully, he wouldn't go digging around into him. That could sink everything he was working on right now and with what happened with him and Meghan, he was in no hurry to leave town—something he'd have to do if Andrew got wind of what he was doing.

On the street, headed to his car, he glanced around, his heart jumping when he saw Meghan entering the Kelly diner. He headed toward the eatery, intent on having a talk with her. She wouldn't be able to avoid him, not with people around.

Inside, he found her standing at the front counter, a twenty-dollar bill in her hand. Was she picking up breakfast for her and Lyle?

She spotted him and her face lost any color that was there. Why was she so upset about seeing him? Did she regret their night together that much?

"Hello. Did you come in to get breakfast?"

She nodded and looked away. She was going to try to ignore him. Boy was that not going to work.

"Can I talk to you for a few minutes?" he asked, moving closer to her. She wasn't going to get away without answering him.

She turned back to him. "I don't have time right now. I must get back to work."

"Okay. Can we talk after work? I can take you out to dinner."

"I don't think that's such a good idea."

"Really? Why's that?"

"Here's your order, Meghan," a dark-haired woman said, diverting her attention to the waitress. She handed her the money and got her change.

"Look, I gotta go."

She attempted to move around him, but he stopped her by reaching out and grasping her forearm.

"Let me buy you dinner and we can talk."

"All right. We can meet at Spencer's Grill at seven. I must go. Lyle can't handle the pharmacy on his own."

"Okay. I'll be there." Jake watched her leave, taking in a frustrated breath. He couldn't wait to sit down and have a meal with her again. She was the only thing that made this whole undercover crap worth it.

Unfortunately, she wasn't the reason he was here—that was to get a story to clear his name. He'd do well to remember that.

****

Meghan glanced at the clock on the wall and wished she had more time. She needed to meet Jackson in twenty minutes and the walk to Spencer's grill would take up five of them. Why had she agreed to have dinner with him since she could barely look him in the eye. Would he be able to see what she was determined to hide? She wasn't sure she was going to tell him about her condition, though how she'd hide it after a certain point was going to be a problem. A man like him being a father to a child of hers wasn't optimal. Could she allow that when he belonged to a hate group? She hardly wanted a child of hers being brought up like that. She knew from experience how close-minded people with certain ideologies could be and she didn't want that for her kid.

Tonight, she was going to have to make him understand she didn't want to see him again. That what they'd shared was not going to be repeated no matter how appealing the man was in her eyes. It was just too dangerous a path.

She took one last look in the mirror and left the spare bedroom of Lily's house, running into her friend on the way to the front door.

"So, what are you going to do?" Lily asked.

"I'm going to tell him I don't think we should see each other anymore."

Her friend frowned. "Are you sure about that? It'll be hard to raise a child on your own, Meghan. What about your dream of becoming a pharmacist? How can you do that as a single mom."

"Women manage to do it every day. It just might take me a year or two longer."

"Lyle isn't a spring chicken, Meghan. He's going to need someone to take over soon."

"Look, I'm going to be late. We can talk about this when I get back?"

"Of course. Do you need a ride?"

"No. I'm going to walk. I need some fresh air. I'll see you later."

Meghan grabbed her purse and the house key Lily had given her and started down the walkway to the street. Hopefully, the short trip to the café would give her time to figure out what she was going to say. She needed to be direct and to the point. Too bad her heart wasn't really in it. Yes, Jackson was a member of BWN but the time they'd spent together had been memorable to say the least. He'd always been kind and respectful to her and to the people around her. If she hadn't known he was staying at the compound on the edge of town, she would've never guessed he was a part of that group. Quite the contradiction. Yet, he was, so that didn't really matter.

On the sidewalk in front of Spencer's Grill, she sighed and stepped inside, squinting at the florescent lighting from above. She spotted Jackson sitting in the back, her heartrate instantly picking up speed. Just the sight of him did strange things to her body. Make her tingle all over. Somehow, she had to fight those feelings, or she'd be lost.

Meghan quickly made her way to the booth and slid in across from him. She was going to make this quick and simple. Make her case and leave.

"Would you like something to drink?" he asked, his

deep baritone sending an electrical impulse ratcheting down her backbone. *Damn him.* Even his voice caused a reaction. Now, she had to keep him from talking, otherwise she may change her mind about ending things tonight.

"Just some ice water, thanks." As cold as possible.

He quickly signaled for the waitress who immediate returned with a large glass filled to the brim.

Meghan took a large swallow, relieved that it helped her dry throat.

He pointed to the menu tucked into a metal stand with sugar packets, as well as a salt and pepper shaker.

"I hear the barbeque chicken is really good," he said.

The mere idea for something so spicy made her stomach revolt. "I'm not planning on staying to eat. I came as a curtesy. We are very different people, Jackson. I don't see a way to continue anything here with us."

The look in his eyes tore at her emotionally. He looked hurt and that was the last think Meghan wanted.

"How are we so different?"

"I don't agree with the people you associate with. The things you believe disturb me. Hate is never a good thing, and I just don't want anything to do with that."

He seemed as if he wanted to object, but instead looked away.

She took another long drink, her nerves getting the better of her. If she didn't leave soon, she was going to break down in front of him and everyone else in the restaurant. She just couldn't allow that to happen. "I think its best I leave, and if I could ask a favor of you, please don't come into Strom anymore. I would appreciate that."

"Yeah, sure. No problem," he said in a harsher tone,

his gaze having darkened.

Meghan rose, and on shaky legs, made her way to the exit. Regret filled her, even though she knew this was the right thing to do. It still didn't make it easy considering she was carrying his child inside her—one that would never know him. Then again, if he knew the truth, he wouldn't let her walk away and she needed him to no matter how painful that was for them both.

Chapter Sixteen

Jake woke from a restless sleep and rolled to his side, unsure of the time since his room had no windows. It could still be early morning. One thing was for sure, his gut still twinged at the thought of what Meghan had said to him at Spencer's last night. Pretty much told him to fuck off forever.

Don't come into Strom's again.

Why didn't she want to see him anymore? What had he done to deserve that? It didn't make any sense.

Okay, so maybe it did.

He shoved the covers on his bed aside and rose, scrubbing the heels of his hands into his eyes. He was lucky if he got two hours of sleep.

Jake padded to his dresser and pulled out a change of clothes, grabbed his shaving kit from the top, and headed down the hall to the communal bathroom to take a shower. Inside, he was relieved to find he was alone. There wasn't anyone beside Cullen who was even worth talking to at the compound. No wonder Meghan didn't want anything to do with him since she thought he was one of them. Would she change her mind if she knew the truth? Would it be worth telling her who he really was?

Maybe it was all for the best. Once he had his story, he'd be leaving anyway, and she'd just be a loose end to tie up. Too bad he didn't think of her in that way. She was so much more than he wanted to admit.

130

He stripped off his boxers and stepped into the shower, his body wash clutched in one hand, a towel in the other. Jake turned the faucet on and allowed the water to course over his head and back, hoping it would relieve all the tension in his body.

A thump from behind had him grabbing for his towel he'd draped over the top of the concrete wall and wrapping it around his waist. Another noise alerted him that whatever it was had moved closer.

"Whose there?" he said in a sharp tone, quickly turning off the water to listen.

No answer.

"Is someone out there?"

Still nothing.

He tightened his hold on the now wet towel and stepped around the concrete stall, his gaze connecting with Andrew, who stood leaning against the wall.

"You scared the shit out of me." Jake swallowed the lump of dread in his throat.

Andrew didn't say anything, just stood there staring at him.

"Did you need something?"

"One of the boys said they saw you with Meghan last night at Spencer's. I told them that couldn't possibly be true since I told you to stay away from her."

Shit. Jake was in deep trouble now. What was he going to say to get him out of this one?

"I was there eating, and she came by to say hello. That was all. She stayed all of five minutes." It wasn't a lie. That was as brief as it was.

Andrew's eyes narrowed. "It wasn't some sort of a date?"

"No. Like I said, it was no more than a hello and

goodbye."

The man pushed away from the wall. "Good. Because you know Felix would murder you in your sleep if he thought you were messing around with her."

"Yeah, I know that. No worries. Can I finish my shower now?"

"Meet me in the dining room when you're finished, and we'll have breakfast together."

"Give me twenty minutes and I'll be there."

Andrew turned to leave, and Jake blew out a relieved breath. *Damn.* That was close. Who had been the one to see him with Meghan? Was he being followed? Did they know he'd visited the police station as well?

He stepped back into the shower stall and turned on the faucets. He was seriously going to have to be more careful now, especially when he couldn't be sure who had been at Spencer's last night watching him.

Jake quickly washed his hair and body, cut the spray and used the damp towel to dry off as much as he could. He dressed and walked back to his room to retrieve his boots, wallet and keys. No way was his breakfast going to be anything but stressful. Andrew gave him the chills. Something about the emptiness in the man's eyes. Void of any consciousness. Someone like that had no qualms about people's lives being lost and that didn't sit well with Jake. That was how atrocities happened in the past, people being led by men like Andrew Gibson.

Jake shook off the thought and made his way to the dining hall, surprised that it was almost empty, only Andrew and Felix's buddy sat at a table, their heads held close together, in an intense conversation. Both men spotted him and pulled back. Jake would have loved to know what they were talking about.

He went to the mess table and grabbed a mug, filled it with coffee and joined the two.

Before he could even take a sip of the brew, he was punched in the arm, causing him to slop some of the coffee onto the table. He grimaced and scowled at Rim. "What the fuck?"

"Can't take a hit, Gallagher? You need to toughen up, man."

Jake refused to be goaded. The guy was itching for a fight and Jake refused to oblige. The last thing he needed was another hit to the head—one pounding headache a month was enough for him.

"I'll have to do that." He plastered a smile on his face.

Both men laughed, which relieved the tension.

Jake had a sneaking suspicion this had been some kind of test and he'd passed it. Too bad it just made him angrier. The games played by this group were childish and grotesque and the sooner he could get out of here the better off he'd be.

****

"Are you sure you don't want me to come with you, Meghan?" Lily asked for the third time that night. "It might not be safe to go alone."

"I'm just going to run out to the house and pick up a few things. I shouldn't be gone longer than an hour."

Lily didn't look relieved by her words, but shrugged and said, "All right. As long as you're sure."

Meghan squeezed her friend's arm. "I am. So, stop worrying."

Lily stepped out of the way and allowed Meghan to leave. She did appreciate her friend's concern, but she couldn't become one of those people who were afraid of her shadow. She'd hate living like that.

Outside, she inhaled a cleansing breath and walked to her car. The trip out to her house should be short and simple. She needed to pick up a few clothes and collect her mail. There were probably bills she needed to pay, and with a week of being at Lily's, the mail was probably piling up.

She drove straight out of town, lucky she only had to stop once at a red light. Mile after mile had her thinking about her conversation with Jackson. It'd been so easy to tell him goodbye, yet not thinking about him hadn't been nearly as simple to do.

When she turned into the driveway, all kinds of memories of him bombarded her. Thank God she wasn't there to stay, otherwise it'd drive her crazy.

She exited the car and hurried inside, thinking it best to get in and out in record time.

On the floor in front of the door were a handful of mail, one letter catching her eye. She reached down and studied the handwriting. It looked vaguely familiar, but she couldn't quite place why, and Meghan really didn't have time to look since Lily expected her back in an hour.

She gathered the rest of the mail, stuffed it into her purse, and walked to her bedroom to round up the stuff she'd need for the next week. Thirty minutes later, she was locking the front door and heading back to her car, intent on putting the past behind her. She may be expecting Jackson's child, but he didn't need to know that, at least not any time soon. Maybe never.

The drive back to town was a little less troubling. Yes, life was going to change but it could be a good thing. One thing was for sure, she'd always put her child before any man. She was doing that by letting Jackson go. Unlike her mother, who would've been better off if she had said goodbye to her father. Supporting a drunk was expensive, money that could have made her mother and her life easier. Meghan would never understand why she'd made that choice. Maybe one day she'd ask her.

Back in town, she parked in front of Lily's house, noticing a strange pickup parked in the driveway. Funny, her friend hadn't said anything about expecting company. Who could it be?

The closer she got to the door, the more the hairs on the back of her neck charged. Something didn't feel right. Maybe she should call Lily before she stepped inside, find out who the visitor was.

Meghan's mouth went dry, and she swallowed hard, her mind going haywire. What the hell was she doing? Too afraid to go inside. This was not who she was.

With trembling fingers, she grabbed the door handle and turned the knob, stepping into the house, listening intently for any voices.

"Lily," she called out, and waited in the foyer for a reply.

"We're in the kitchen."

Meghan walked through the hallway to the back. The kitchen was off to the right side of the home.

When she entered, a blond man stood next to Lily with his back to Meghan.

"Look who showed up to see you." Lily smiled at her. "He said he was an old friend."

The guy turned and all the blood drained from Meghan's body, leaving a cold chill in its wake.

"Hey, sweetheart. How is my girl doing?" His evil

eyes roamed over her like a predator getting ready to attack. The gesture made her skin crawl.

"What are you doing here?"

"I talked to your daddy a few weeks ago and he told me about your so-called husband, which I found out, with a little digging, was a lie you told him. Why would you tell him you were married when you're not?"

"What I tell my father is none of your business, Tom."

"That's not quite true, Meghan. Your daddy and I had a verbal agreement that you were to marry me. You defaulted on that by running away. I expect you to abide by the agreement or I'll have to have your father pay for said default, or should I say your mother since that daddy of yours hasn't worked in ages."

Meghan's jaw slackened and she glared back at him. "You have no right to bring my mother into this. She never agreed to our union and neither did I."

"Doesn't matter. There were several in attendance when the agreement was made. Liquor ain't cheap you know, and your daddy seems to need it at this point. Money changed hands and sealed the deal. You are mine, like it or not."

Meghan was mortified. She had no idea her father had been paid to take her. She would never forgive him—not ever.

"I'm not a head of cattle. People can't be bought. I'm not going to marry you no matter what you say or do."

"Suit yourself. You know Sheriff Alberts, right? He's a friend of mine. A close friend. I'll give him a call when I get home and have him take care of this. I'd hate for rumors to get your mother fired. At her age, it might be hard for her to find another job, don't you think?"

Meghan's eyes filled with tears. She couldn't believe this was happening. Was she going to have to pack up and leave again—hide until this disgusting man gave up and married someone else?

"I'll give you a few hours to think about this, Meghan. I'm staying at the Brookville Motel. Come by and give me an answer. I'll be leaving in the morning."

She watched him exit the door and looked over at her friend whose eyes were wide as saucers. "I'm so sorry, Meghan. He said he was a friend from your hometown. If I'd have known—"

Meghan raised a hand to stop her from finishing her response. "You didn't know. It's okay. I'll deal with this. Don't worry."

"So, this is why you left?"

Meghan nodded. "Yes."

"What are you going to do?"

What was she going to do? Meghan wasn't sure. Running away was one option, but there was another possibility. That one could solve her problem if she could make it happen. Too bad she didn't know if she could, and she had only a few hours to find out.

Chapter Seventeen

Jake spent the day looking over his shoulder. Someone could very well be following him around and he was determined to find out either way. All morning, he'd caught Andrew watching him and it literally gave him the chills. He couldn't take it any longer. He needed to get out of the compound for a few hours and recharge his batteries.

He'd find an empty coffee shop and try to unwind, consider if this whole thing was worth it. If he wasn't concerned about what Andrew was up to, he'd pack his stuff and get out of here. But how could he do that when something was afoot. He could be the catalyst to saving lives. So, right now, even if he wanted to leave, he couldn't. Besides, he still had to deal with Meghan.

As he drove, the simple image of her took his breath. There was something about her that left him feeling confused, made him irritated, yet he wanted her like no other. She made him experience emotions he'd never felt before.

He pulled up in front of the twenty-four-hour diner, killed the engine and jumped out. Inside, he walked to the booth he'd occupied a few nights ago.

A waitress came over. "What can I get you?"

"Coffee, thanks."

Jake shifted in the seat, trying to calm his frazzled nerves. When she returned with his coffee, the door jingled, and he looked up to see Meghan heading his way. The sight of her made his heart miss a much-needed beat. For whatever reason, he knew she'd be his undoing.

"Can I join you?"

He nodded. "Of course. Do you want some coffee?"

"No. I need to ask you a question."

"Okay." He sat back and waited for her to proceed.

Meghan paused for the waitress to leave after telling her she didn't need anything.

Minute after minute ticked by, and the longer she remained quiet, the more anxious Jake became.

"I need a favor, Jackson."

Jake watched her tear at the napkin on the table and knew what she was about to ask made her more anxious than she appeared.

"What do you need, Meghan?" he prompted when she looked like she was getting ready to bolt.

She looked him straight in the eye. "I need you to marry me."

Jake's jaw dropped open. "You need me to what?"

"Just temporarily." Her eyes left his and wandered around the room.

He had no idea what was going on, but he needed her to explain.

"Why do you need me to marry you temporarily, Meghan? I don't understand."

"You can just say no," she shot back, looking on the verge of tears.

"Whoa, wait a minute." He reached across the table and covered her arm with his hand. "I didn't say I wouldn't. I asked why you needed me to."

"Remember that we told my father we were married?"

"Sure, yeah."

"Well, he told someone, and the man came to see me today. He knows we lied to my father. He wants me to marry him because of an agreement my father and he made. I can't, Jackson. He's a horrible man. I need you to do this for me. Please."

Jake frowned. The whole thing made no sense. "And you can't tell him no."

"He threatened to get my mother fired from a job she's had for twenty-plus years. At her age, she'd never be able to find another one. She supports her and my father."

What a fucking asshole. Who would force someone to marry them? *A disgusting human-being, that's who.*

"I need him to see we have no future together, and you and I can end our marriage quietly."

Jake stared at her, not sure what to do. He could marry her, but it wouldn't be legal using his alias. If he said yes, he was going to have to tell her the truth about why he was there. At that point she'd be involved in the ruse, a situation he really didn't want to put her in. Yet, it sounded like he had no choice.

"I'm afraid it's my turn to tell you something, Meghan. You may not want to marry me after you hear what."

Her eyes widened and she shifted against the back of the booth seat. "What's that?"

Jake swallowed hard. "First, you need to promise not to tell anyone what I'm about to tell you."

"Okay. I promise," she said in a shaky voice.

Jake studied her reaction. He really didn't have a choice. He was going to have to trust her. "My name isn't Jackson Gallagher. It's Jake Mills and I'm a reporter. I'm working uncover on a story about White Supremacy. It took me weeks to get in and I can't have my cover blown. Do you understand that?"

Meghan nodded, though he could see she was shocked by his confession.

"Are you sure you still want to do this?" Jake knew it was a lot to comprehend in such a short time.

"I do. Are you saying yes?"

"Yes. I'll marry you and if you want me to talk to this guy, I will. But we need to do it somewhere else. Not here in town. I can't let Andrew get wind of it, or Felix for that matter. You could be a widow the same day you were a wife."

"That's fine with me. I'd like to keep it quiet as well. I do have to tell you, I'm glad to hear you aren't a part of that group."

"I imagine so. When do you want to do this?"

"To be honest, as soon as possible. Tom expects an answer in a few hours."

"Is that even possible?"

"Yes. If we hurry, we can get a license and get hitched if someone is available to marry us. We could get it done at the courthouse in Madison."

"Let's get going. Is there anything I'll need?"

"Driver's license I believe and a birth certificate."

Jake was just lucky he had both hidden in his SUV in case he was ever pulled over.

"I got it. Let's take my car."

She reached over and squeezed his arm. "Thank you, Jacks…Jake."

"Don't thank me yet. If we don't hurry, it might not happen."

****

On the ride back from Madison, Meghan twisted the ring on her finger that they'd purchased at a box store in the neighboring town, still unsure if she had made the right decision. It was impulsive, yes, but what other choice did she have. Tom had threatened retaliation. This seemed to be her only option. Hopefully, he'd understand striking back now would do no good.

She glanced over at the man driving who made this all possible. Just looking at him made her heart flutter, especially when she knew he was working a story and wasn't a real member of the BWN. A shocking revelation to be sure.

He turned her way, his brow furrowed. "Having any regrets about what we did?"

"Not yet," she said. "How about you?"

"Haven't really had time to think about it. You need me to talk to this Tom fellow for you? Send him on his way?"

"I can deal with him. It's sweet of you to offer, though."

"Do you want me to take you to your friends or were you supposed to meet this guy somewhere?"

"Just drop me off at Lily's. He told me where he was staying. If nothing else, I'll go there.

He frowned. "Will Lily be there? I really don't want you alone with him."

Meghan was touched by his concern. "I imagine she will. You don't need to worry."

"You're my wife now. It comes with territory."

She couldn't help but laugh. For whatever reason, him calling her his wife sounded nice, even if it was a temporary thing. And the cherry on top was that now her child would have his name.

Should she tell him? Somehow, she knew now wasn't the right time. She had other things to deal with. Maybe when they saw each other again. If she worked up the nerve.

When they pulled up in front of Lily's, her confidence waned. Was this going to work? Suddenly, she wasn't so sure.

With a shaky hand, Meghan reached for the door handle and was about to get out of his SUV when he clasped her forearm to stop her. "Are you sure you don't want me to take care of this?"

She shook her head. "I think he'll be more willing to listen to reason from me. But thank you for offering."

"Can we see each other tomorrow? I'd like to know what he says."

"I have to work but we can meet for lunch."

"Okay. Where you want to eat?"

"I'm not sure we should be seen in public. Someone might tell Felix. How about I make a picnic lunch and you come into the pharmacy? We can eat in the back."

"And Lyle will be okay with that?"

"Yes. I'll see you around eleven?"

He smiled, gracing her with those beautiful white teeth. Her stomach clenched and she took a breath. Meghan needed to get out of there before she leaned over and kissed his amazing mouth.

"Bye." She opened the door and exited. The man had becoming all consuming, especially now that she knew he was a good man. Maybe, just maybe, he'd also be a good father.

Shaking the thought, she entered the house and searched for her friend. She found Lily in the kitchen, at the stove, cooking dinner. Her face was awash with concern when she saw Meghan. "Where did you go. I was starting to worry."

"I had to talk to someone who could help get rid of Tom."

Lily turned to look at her. "Did you find this person?"

"I did. I think I solved my problem."

"Wonderful. What's the plan?"

Meghan wasn't sure if she should divulge what she'd done, though her friend would eventually find out.

"What did you do?" Lily asked in a blunt voice when she didn't answer.

"I'll tell you, but you can't say anything to anyone. Not ever. Can you do that?"

"Oh my God, Meghan, you're scaring me. What have you done?"

She hesitated for a moment, then held out her left hand, the ring in full view.

Lily's eyes widened. "You got engaged? Wait, that ring is on the wrong…did you get married?"

Meghan nodded. "I did."

"Who did you marry?"

"Really?" Meghan frowned at her best friend. "Who do you think!"

"Jackson? Did you get hitched to Gallagher?"

"Yes. But don't tell anyone. It could be life or death for him."

"I don't get it. Why would he agree to that with such high stakes?"

"Because he doesn't want Tom to have a hold on me and I appreciate that."

"Did you tell him about the baby?"

For whatever reason, Lily appeared angry at what

she'd done and, for the life of her, she had no idea why. "I haven't yet but I will when the time is right. I wanted to take care of this thing with Tom first."

"So, you will tell him?"

"Yes, I will. Why all the concern about Jackson?"

Her friend shrugged. "I don't know. I just think that with him doing this for you, you owe him that."

"You're right," Meghan said in a sharper voice than she meant to. But this whole thing was starting to feel strange to her. What was Lily's real reason for wanting her to tell Jake she was pregnant? Did she think it'd change everything—that he'd walk away? The thought made her stomach revolt. She swallowed the bile working up her throat. She hadn't planned to tell him yet, but would he be angry with her? Would he leave her there to deal with the consequences? He wasn't staying in town. He was here for a story. Once that was finished, he'd be gone.

Perhaps telling him wasn't such a great idea after all.

A knock at the door brought Meghan back to the present.

She headed to the front. It had to be Tom and she needed to formulate what she was going to say. Best to just come out and tell him that she and Jackson were married and that he could go and fuck himself. Maybe not use those words since it'd probably get her slapped.

With her head held high, she turned the knob and opened the door, the smug look on her ex's face making her want to smack him. God, she hated this man and everything he stood for.

"Are you ready to concede?"

"Hardly. I'm not going to let you blackmail me, Tom." She held out her hand. "Jackson and I got married.

You have no ties to me. If you try to ruin my parents' lives, I'll contact the church and tell them what you were trying to do. You may have a lot of clout there, but they might not like blackmail. You could likely get removed from your job."

His eyes turned pitch black and Meghan stepped back.

"Okay, Meghan, you won this round. When you least expect it, the next will be mine. Watch your back, babe." He swiveled on this heel and took off down the driveway to his car.

For what seemed like an eternity, she stared at his retreating car, too emotional to do anything else. Here, she thought he'd see reason, but it was clear this was some kind of game to him—one he refused to lose.

Chapter Eighteen

The whole evening and next morning Jake had been worried about Meghan's meeting with this Tom character. The guy sounded like a real loser, one who was willing to do anything to get what he wanted. A lot like Andrew and Felix. There seemed to be a bunch who fit that particular mold. Were these sub-humans being churned out in large numbers somewhere? Or was Jake somehow drawn into their dark realm?

Most of this troubling day he'd spent in his room, leaving only long enough to get a mug of coffee. He'd been more than thankful no one stopped to talk to him, all seeming to shy away with him being the new guy. Jake was more than okay with that. These people weren't anyone he wanted to get to know anyway.

Hell, he simply wanted to be with Meghan. Crazy, yes, but she had taken up residence in his brain and he couldn't shake her out, no matter how hard he tried.

They were married after all. She was tied to him and instead of feeling trapped or somehow stifled, he felt exhilarated to see what his future would hold if she gave them a real chance. He couldn't wait to introduce her to his mother and sister. Somehow, he knew they'd love her.

But what if he couldn't talk her into giving their relationship a fighting chance? What if she flat-out said goodbye? What would he do? He certainly wouldn't want to hang on to someone who didn't want to stay with him. No way would he force her to care about him because of a deal they'd stuck.

Jake shook off the negativity. He had enough of that here at the compound. He still had a job to do right now, and he needed to learn what Andrew was up to with the guy at the insurance company and that local farmer. What could be the connection? What were the three planning?

How could he find out? Maybe a little spying on Andrew was in order? It could be Jake's only option. Though, Cullen might have learned something since they last spoke. He needed to talk to him first.

Jake rose from his bed. He had to find him and see if anything had changed.

Down the hall, as he headed toward the living area, he ran into Felix who sneered and stomped by him. What he wouldn't give to be able to return Felix's favor and whack him upside his brainless head. *Fucking POS!*

After a fifteen-minute search for Cullen, Jake came up short. He was nowhere around. Perhaps Andrew knew where he'd gone. Maybe he had sent him into town for something.

He retraced his step down the long hallway and overheard voices coming from inside the boss's office.

"Where is he?" Andrew asked in a low voice.

"Best you not know."

"Shit. We are going to have to up our timeline on our plans. If we don't do this soon, we're going to get found out and stopped."

Jake's stomach lurched. What the hell was this dude planning and who was the guy who Andrew shouldn't know anything about? Did they find out Cullen was here undercover? Was he okay? Jake had to find him. But how?

He headed for the front door to see if Cullen's Harley was outside. If it wasn't, he'd go searching in town. If it was, he'd turn the compound upside down, all the while trying not to get noticed while doing it.

He looked around the parking lot, no sign of Cullen's bike.

Relief had him blowing out a breath. So, he could be running an errand. Jake was going to find him because something big was about to go down and Cullen and the ATF needed to know.

He quickly jumped in his SUV and hooked his seatbelt in place as he was leaving the compound. He took Main Street, looking left to right, losing patience when he came up short again. No sign of Cullen's Harley anywhere. Could he be meeting with a fellow officer out of town? Jake hoped that was the case.

Instead of heading back to the compound, he turned into the alley between Markley's Hardware store and Strom's pharmacy and parked next to his wife's car. Just thinking that Meghan was his made him smile. He couldn't wait to see her, to find out how her meeting went.

Inside the side door, he glanced around, spotting Meghan in an aisle placing medication on one of the shelves. Again, her skin looked pasty white. What was going on with her? Was she sick, or just upset with what happened the night before?

He strode up the aisle and stopped a few feet away, studying her profile. Even with her waning color she was exquisite. So beautiful, she took his breath.

He reached out, brushed a finger across her wrist

and she jumped, her green eyes widening. "I dropped by to find out how it went with Tom last night. Did he leave town?"

She shrugged. "I have no idea. I'm not sure my plan worked. He didn't seem all that fazed by my announcement. He told me I needed to watch my back."

"Do you know where he was staying?"

"No idea. Just let it go, Jake. You'll just make things worse."

"I don't like you and Lily being at the house alone with that creep lurking around. Let me come stay with you or we could both stay at your house and leave Lily out of this altogether."

She sighed deeply. "That would be hard for you since you're here in Brooksville on a story. I'd just get in the way of that."

He pulled her close. "No one is more important to me right now than you."

She started to say something but shook her head instead. "I'll be fine. Lily and I are only a minute away from the police station. If I feel threatened in any way, I'll let you know. Get what you need to write that article. If anyone needs to be exposed it's the BWN."

Jake wanted to object but he knew from the look of determination on her face, she wasn't going to budge on this. "All right. I'm going to run and get a cell phone and come back and give you the number. I want you to call me if anything happens. Okay?"

She nodded. "I promise."

"You haven't seen Cullen Hatfield today, have you?"

"I haven't. Why?"

"I just need to talk to him, and he was gone this

morning when I got up."

"If I see him, I'll tell him you're looking for him."

"I'd appreciate that. I'm going to be back soon with that number. Can we do that lunch you mentioned yesterday?"

"Yes. Can you pick something up? I can't leave since Lyle had a doctor's appointment."

"Is he doing okay?" There was something so likeable about the old man that Jake cared about him, especially since he brought Meghan and him together.

She smiled. "It's an annual checkup. He's doing fine. Even he needs to see a doctor to get his medications refilled."

"What do you feel like eating for lunch?"

She shrugged. "Surprise me."

"I'll be back in a few hours."

"All right." Suddenly she looked nervous.

Why was she anxious? He'd love to know but right now he needed to get a burner phone. He touched her arm and turned to leave.

Later, he'd ask her, and hopefully, she'd trust him enough to tell him the truth.

****

Meghan had spent the morning with a churning in her stomach that was worse than ever before. She'd been thankful that Jake hadn't hung around any longer than he had because she couldn't deal with the nausea and the feeling that seeing him caused in her gut. It didn't help her situation at all. She still couldn't believe he'd offered to completely tank his chances at a story for her. What did that mean? Did he really care about her? Was her safety paramount to him like he'd said?

The door opening had her shaking off his comments.

She looked over to see who'd entered, her blood instantly chilling at the sight of Tom. He moved toward her, and she froze. "What are you doing here?" she asked when he was within a few feet of her.

"Did you think I was leaving town?"

"There's no reason for you to stay."

"Potayto, potahto. I kind of like it here. By the way, I saw your husband leaving. Handsome guy if you're into that dark, brooding crap. Not anywhere near as good looking as I am, of course. Adonis comes to mind when I look in a mirror."

Meghan laughed. The man was delusional in every way.

"Then you'll have no problem finding another woman to fall at your feet. You need to go look for that lady since it isn't me. Now, go away. I'm working."

"I could but I don't want anyone else. Nothing and *no one* is going to get in my way, Meghan."

The threat was clear as day. Was he planning to hurt Jake? What could he possibly do? Here, Jake was worried about her. Now, she had to be worried about him. Maybe they did need to stay together to protect each other.

When he returned with that phone number and to do lunch, she'd insist on staying at her place with him. With Meghan not staying with Lily, surely her friend would be safer.

With that settled, she turned and left Tom standing in the aisle. She was finished talking to him. Done trying to make him see reason. The man was delusional and there was no dealing with that.

Meghan stepped behind the counter as the doorbell signaled his departure, causing her to blow out a strangled breath. She slowly counted to ten, trying to dissipate the anger building inside of her. This was exactly why she left Abbott in the first place. She knew this man could never make her happy and she refused to be tied to him. Now, Jake was an altogether different animal. He made her feel things she'd never felt before and being his wife, if only by name, somehow felt right.

Lyle stepped in from the back and brought her back to her job. She still had a half a box of medications to price and shelf, and she needed to do it before Jake returned.

"How'd your doctor's appointment go? Is everything okay?" she asked him.

He gave her a weak smile. "Don't worry yourself about me, missy. I'm fine. You, though, look pale again today. Are you taking those vitamins I gave you?"

"I am. Mornings have been rough."

"You need to get yourself down to the doctor's office and get a checkup."

Lyle was right, of course. She did need a doctor to confirm her condition, but would it stay between her and the doctor? She couldn't allow this to spread to people in town. She needed time to figure out her plans first.

"I will soon, Lyle. I promise. Would it be all right if Jak…Jackson and I do lunch in the back?" Meghan just about blew it and called him Jake. She needed to be more careful, though she was sure she could trust her boss not to say anything.

Lyle frowned and Meghan knew why. He believed the worst about Jake being part of that hate group, especially after picking up that drug used to make Meth, and right now it wasn't a good time to set him straight.

"Are you sure you want to do this?"

"I am. He's been good to me. I think you need to give him the benefit of the doubt."

Maybe she could make him see reason without having to reveal anything.

"Okay. I trust your judgement, Meghan, and under the circumstances, it might be a good idea to allow him into your life. Have you told him anything yet?"

"No. I'm not ready to do that. I'd appreciate you not saying anything either."

His mouth curved into a grin. "You know me better than that. My lips are sealed."

"I need to get back to work. He'll be here," she said, glancing up at the clock. "In about an hour, and I still have half a box of vitamins to stock and another of paper produces to put out. I better get on that."

"Pace yourself, girlie. You don't want to get all light-headed again."

"I promise, I'll be careful. I have more than myself to think about now." Once the words left her mouth, reality hit her like a ton of bricks. Her life was no longer her own—another life depended on her, and she needed to come to terms with that.

Chapter Nineteen

What Jake had to do had taken longer than he'd expected since he had to avoid one of the men from the compound who'd been lurking inside the store. So, he'd had to wait until the creep left to get a phone and minutes installed. There was no reason to get another plan when he already had one at home.

He pulled into the drive-thru and ordered enough food for Meghan, Lyle and himself. He needed to get back on the good side of her boss since he knew how much Strom meant to her.

Jake quickly paid for the food, placed the bags beside him and drove back to the pharmacy, eager to see Meghan again. Damned if he wasn't smitten with her.

In the back parking area, he made a beeline for inside. Immediately, he heard a voice that caused him to back up. What was Andrew Gibson doing here, talking to Meghan?

He slid behind a shelf and listened.

"What are you trying to insinuate?" she asked in a voice that made the hairs on the back of Jake's neck stand up.

"Rumor has it you've been dating Jackson Gallagher. I'm just asking if that's true."

Jesus Christ! Why was Andrew here asking Meghan about him? This wasn't good. Andrew knew something or he wouldn't be there. This whole thing was starting to unravel, and he needed to get out while he still could.

He eased out of his hiding place and exited the pharmacy. He was going to go pack his shit and hide out somewhere. Meghan had Lyle and customers, including a deputy in the corner, to sideline Andrew. No way would he try anything when the store was filled with people. Once he was clear of the compound, he'd call her and let her know he wouldn't be back for lunch. If he stayed in Brookville, everything he did would have to been done covertly.

He sped into the compound and took the back entrance into the kitchen, relieved that no one was around. Knowing Andrew, everyone was probably on the lookout for him.

He snuck down the hallway to his room and threw everything in his bag, including the notebook with all his research, and retraced his steps back to the kitchen, quickly leaving again. Jake was damn lucky he was able to get in and out without being noticed.

In his SUV, his mind started to turn. Where could he stay so that no one would find him? The motels in town would be the first places Andrew and his goons would look. He couldn't stay there or at Lily's. That would only put them at risk.

But he could stay at Meghan's house, out of town, away from prying eyes. And he knew where she kept the spare key. He'd lay low out there until dark and decide what to do next.

With that idea formulated, he turned left and headed out of town. Hopefully, even if he had to drive to Carson to get supplies, this plan would work. First, he'd call Meghan, tell her what was happening. After, he'd find Cullen. The man not being around that morning had Jake nervous, worried for his safety and finding him was paramount. Did the man have to check in with his fellow officers daily? Weekly? Would they come looking for him if he didn't? Should Jake try to get word to them about his concerns? He wished he knew.

Though, this could be as simple as Cullen just wasn't around when Jake got up.

He drove into the driveway behind Meghan's house to hide his vehicle. He didn't want anyone driving by knowing he was here.

He cut the engine, grabbed the takeout bags, and headed for the front door, stopping only long enough to retrieve the key under the large rock in an array of them next to the kitchens window.

After unlocking the door, he quickly stepped inside, sent the bolt lock in place and inhaled a deep breath. Now, he could relax for a while. No one would have any idea he was here.

He turned and glanced around, memories of his time with Meghan overtaking him. How had she managed to work her way into his heart in such a short time? In all these years, Jake had only focused on his career, dating here and there, but never allowing any woman to detract from his purpose. Until now. Until Meghan had opened his eyes to what really was important. Finding someone to love. But did she feel the same? He had no idea.

He strode into the kitchen and placed the bags on the table. He'd eat something. Afterwards, he'd try to find Strom's number in Meghan's stuff and call her. What he wouldn't give to have her here right now, but that wouldn't be safe for her. She was better off at Lily's, and he was going to make sure she stayed there for now.

****

Meghan held onto her temper until Andrew walked out the door, her anger so intense she wanted to scream. "That man had a lot of nerve asking me any personal questions, especially about my love life." No way would she ever tell him. Who was he to even ask?

"You need to calm down, girlie, or you are going to make yourself sick," Lyle said, placing a reassuring hand on her arm and giving her that stern look of his.

"I know but he had no reason to come here and ask me if I was dating Jackson. What is it to him, anyway?"

"That bunch ain't nothing but trouble. I should ban them all from coming in here."

Meghan had to agree but all that would do was cause problems for Lyle and he didn't need that.

She glanced at the clock on the wall and noticed how late Jake was. Why wasn't he here yet.

"Looks like your fellow is a no show. You want to run out and get us something to eat?"

Meghan looked at the clock again. Jake would have been here by now if he was coming.

"Okay. What do you feel like today?"

The old man smiled. "How about you surprise me."

"Okay, but remember I asked." Meghan gave him a wink for good measure.

"Go on now. Get out of here. My stomach is gnawing a hole in itself."

"I'm going." She reached under the counter for her purse, exiting through the side door. She jumped into her car, thinking about where she'd stop, all the while wondering what had happened to Jake. This wasn't like him—not to do what he said he'd do. Then again, did she really know him all that well? True, he wasn't a white supremacist, but did she know anything about Jake

Mills? Who he was as a man? Not really.

She turned onto Main Street and decided to stop at the local deli to pick up a couple of sandwiches, a much healthier option than a greasy burger. Lyle didn't need that at his age. With his heart.

She coasted into a parking spot in front of Hanover's and was getting out when she spotted Cullen coming out of the coffee shop next door. She quickly rushed over to talk to him.

"Hi, Cullen, right?"

"That's me. You're Lily's friend. Meghan?"

"Yes. Have you spoken to Jackson today? He was looking for you earlier."

The man frowned. "No, I haven't seen him."

"Okay. Well, I told him if I saw you to tell you he's looking for you. Wanted to talk to you."

"Do you know why?"

"I have no idea. I just thought I better tell you."

The man smiled. "Thank you. I appreciate that."

"I better get going. Have a nice day."

"You, too."

Meghan left him and headed into the deli, wondering why Jake needed to talk to him. The man was part of BWN. That spelled no good to her.

At the counter, she quickly ordered two club sandwiches, two large pickles and a couple of chocolate chip cookies for dessert. Jake not showing up for lunch was starting to worry her. What if something happened? Could Andrew have found out he was undercover doing a story and decided to do something about it? But, why come in and ask her questions? That didn't make sense if he'd done something to hurt Jake. Unless he was trying to find out what she knew. Somehow, though, she believed it was something else and she'd just have to wait to hear from him.

When her number was called, she quickly grabbed the bag and headed out the door. It took her only a few minutes to get back to the pharmacy. "I hope you like what I picked," she said as she stepped into the side door and started for the counter, her heart skidding to a stop. Lyle lay on the floor, his skin pale, sweat beading on his forehead. Was he breathing? She couldn't tell.

Meghan raced to grab the phone, returned and knelt as she dialed 9-1-1.

When they answered, she said. "I need an ambulance."

"What's wrong?"

"I just found my boss passed out on the ground. He's in his seventies and has heart issues. Please hurry."

"Paramedics are on their way. Can you tell if he's breathing?"

"I think so, yes."

The sound of sirens relieved Meghan. She clasped Lyle's hand and held tight. "You 're going to be all right. Hang on." Tears filled her eyes. She loved this man. He was the only one who felt like family to her. She couldn't lose him.

"Are you inside Strom's pharmacy?" the dispatcher asked.

"Yes," Meghan said.

Lyle started to groan, and his eyes fluttered. "Wh...at happ...ened?" he asked in a weak voice.

"I came in and found you on the floor. You don't remember?"

Paramedics rushed inside the door, came over to them and quickly checked Lyle's vitals, forcing him to stay down when he tried to get up. "Listen to them, Lyle," Meghan said in a sharper than intended tone. "You need to go to the hospital and find out if you're okay. I'll lock up the pharmacy and be right behind you."

He gave her a pitiful look while allowing them to load him onto a gurney and out of the store.

Meghan shoved a tear away and went to lock the back door. They were expecting a delivery in a few hours, and she quickly called the service to rearrange that shipment, set the alarm and locked the front door. She had to get to the hospital. Lyle didn't have any family of his own. She was it and she had to make sure doctors did everything they could to see to it that he returned to life as usual.

Chapter Twenty

Jake punched in the number once again and waited. It rang and rang and rang. "Shit." Why wasn't anyone picking up the phone at the pharmacy? It didn't make any sense. He'd been trying to call for over an hour now with no answer. The line being busy was one thing but not answering at a business during business hours was another.

He placed the phone down on the kitchen table and started to pace, imagining all kinds of horrible things. Andrew Gibson being at the top of that list.

But was he being paranoid? It could be as simple as a phone problem at the store, more likely than where his mind had gone, especially when there had been a police officer in the store when he left.

But all he could do was wait until dark to find out either way.

Jake stopped to stare out the window, angry with himself for not asking for her cell phone number that morning. Hindsight was twenty-twenty. He was paying the price now.

He inhaled a deep breath. *Just stay calm. There isn't anything you can do at this point.*

Frustrated, he pushed away from the window and left the kitchen. He went to sit down on the sofa, laid his head back and closed his eyes, wishing Meghan was with him.

Nope. He couldn't involve her in his mess. That would only put her at risk, and he cared about her too much to do that.

Jake turned his head to the side and his eyes grew heavy. When he finally reopened them, it was dark outside.

He sat up and flinched at the crick in his neck. Great. This was the last thing he needed. In pain, he rose and went to find something to take. Somehow, he was going to go find out why no one was answering the phone at Strom's.

Before leaving the house, he tucked the key in his pocket and turn the lock on the door so that when he closed it would be secured.

He walked around back and headed for his SUV. He wasn't sure where he'd go first. At this time, Meghan would have closed the pharmacy. Would she be at Lily's? Only one way to find out. But he needed to be careful. BWN had a lot of members, and he couldn't be seen by any of them.

In town, he used all back roads to get to Lily's house, parking on a dark side street. He walked to the back door instead of the front, which was lit up by the streetlight.

He knocked and waited. When no one came, he knocked again, finally hearing footsteps nearing. From inside, a curtain was pulled back and moments later the door opened. Lily stood there looking stunned by his presence. "What are you doing here?"

"I needed to talk to Meghan. Is she around?"

Her eyes widened. "So, you don't know?"

"Know what?"

"She's at the hospital."

Jake's stomach made a nosedive. Maybe his initial concerns from earlier were correct, and something terrible happened to her. Did it involve Gibson? "What happened?"

"They think Lyle had a stroke. She's there with him."

He hated to feel relief, but he did. Meghan was all right. "What hospital is he at?"

"Regional over in Emmery."

"Thanks," he said and turned to leave. He'd go see her and find out how Lyle was doing.

On the edge of town, he spotted Cullen's motorcycle parked at the only motel in Brooksville. He pulled in next to the bike and cut the engine. Who was Cullen here to see or did he meet a lady along the way? That could be why he couldn't find him that morning.

How did Jake find out what room he was in? He doubted that the clerk at the counter would give it out freely. Maybe he could bribe him through.

He rushed inside and glanced around, wondering if they charged by the hour.

"Can I help you?" a heavyset guy with a scruffy beard and a balding head asked.

"I noticed Cullen Hatfield's bike out front. Could you tell me what room he's in?"

"Now why would I go and do that?" He stuck a toothpick in his mouth and swirled it around with his fingers.

"Would a twenty talk you into it?" Jake took out his wallet and extracted a crisp bill and waved it at the man.

The guy laughed. "Try again."

He took out another twenty. "How about forty?"

"How about sixty?" the man said, his greenish eyes

taking on an evil glint.

"All right, but you better not give me the wrong room number, or I'll come and get my money back one way or another."

He handed the guy the money. "He's in room sixteen down on the end. He's been there pretty much all day. Though, if I had a hot lady like he had coming in, that's where I be too."

Jake left the office, wondering who this so-called woman could be that Cullen was here with.

He walked down the sidewalk to the end and knocked on the door. The door came open and Jake's jaw slackened. The woman standing there had to be the most exotic creature Jake had seen. Asian descent with the darkest hair. She was dressed in a red tank top and a pair of silk, drawstring pants. "Yes," she said, her voice soft.

"I'm looking for Cullen."

The man instantly stuck his head out the door. "Jake? What are you doing here?"

"I was worried about you. I think I may be in trouble. I was concerned you might be as well."

"Get in here." Cullen grabbed his arm, pulled him into the room and the woman closed the door.

"How do you know you're in trouble?" he asked, his brow furrowing.

"I'm not for sure I am, but I wasn't taking any chances. Andrew was at the pharmacy asking Meghan about our relationship. I don't have any idea how he found out about us."

"Whoa, you and Meghan Gentry are a thing? When did that happen?"

"I wouldn't really call us a thing. But the days I was gone, I was with her." Jake glanced over at the woman, wondering if it was even safe to be telling Cullen what he was in front of her. He pointed at her. "Who is this lovely lady? Friend or something else?"

"Malaysia is ATF. She's my boss, among other things." He smiled at her.

She returned the gesture and turned back to Jake. "Why are you undercover at BWN?"

"Because I need to get this story to return my reputation to a good place. I was named in an article about a year ago as a supporter of this movement. I need to prove I'm not."

"Do you have any idea how dangerous these people are? You could get yourself killed, and no one would be the wiser. We've been following this group along with a string of Militias. All bad. All willing to kill for their cause. I understand your job is important to you, but your life should matter more."

"Why don't you let me help?"

She shook her head. "You need to pack up and leave before you get killed."

"No. Andrew is planning something. This morning, I overheard him talking to Bart. Something about a man who was taken care of. I thought they were talking about you, Cullen. You're okay so it was someone else. That's when Andrew said they were going to need to speed up their plans. Something bad is about to go down. Let me help you find out what before people get hurt."

Cullen rubbed at his jaw, looking more than troubled. "Give us tonight to think about this. Where are you staying now?"

"At Meghan's house. Nobody knows and I'm keeping my truck hidden."

"Meet me here tomorrow night and we'll discuss

this further. In the meantime, lay low and stay safe."

"I will." Jake headed for the door. "You do the same."

****

Meghan waited in the room Lyle had been assigned, thankful for a private room. He'd been taken down for a brain scan twenty minutes earlier and she was waiting for him to return. To say that her nerves were on edge would be an understatement. At least Lyle was coherent and alert and had been since she got to the hospital. That was a relief. But what had caused him to pass out? Hopefully, the scan could tell them something since his EKG looked normal.

A knock at the door caused her to jerk, almost unseating her from her chair. She glanced over to see Jake stepping inside the room, concern evident on his face.

She shouldn't be, but she was happy to see him.

"How's he doing?" he asked, coming to stand next to her.

"Better than he was when I found him. Who told you we were here?"

"I stopped by Lily's, and she told me what happened. I'd been trying to call the pharmacy for hours. I know now why no one answered. How are *you* doing?"

She shrugged. "I'm okay. Worried about Lyle. They took him down for a brain scan since his heart appears okay."

"Do they think he might have had a stroke?"

"I guess that's their thought. I pray it didn't cause any damage."

He squeezed her arm, a reassuring gesture that sent her heart racing in her chest. Why did this man make her feel all warm and fuzzy inside every time he touched her? What was so different about Jake?

"What happened that you didn't show up for lunch?" she asked, still stinging from his absence.

"I did come, had lunch in hand, but Andrew was there asking you those questions. I think he suspects something. I rushed back to the compound and packed up my stuff and got out."

Meghan's stomach dropped. Did this mean he was leaving? Why did the mere thought make her want to cry? Did she care about him? Want him to be a part of her and her child's life? Should she tell him about it? God, she wished she knew what to do. Lyle would but he wasn't here to talk to. "So, what are you going to do?"

"I'm going to lay low for now."

"Where? The motel in town is not a safe place to stay. Andrew has friends in low places and that dive is as low as they go."

"Yeah, I agree. Hope you don't mind but I'm hiding out at your place for now. I remembered where you said you kept a spare key."

"That's fine. As long as you're safe."

A noise from behind had them both turning to see Lyle being wheeled back into the room. Meghan took ahold of Jake's arm and backed them into the corner until they had him hooked up to the monitors and gave him the call button in case he needed anything.

"Maybe I should go," Jake said once the nurses had left.

"No!" Meghan held onto his arm, needing him to stay. He made her feel safe.

"You need to take her home," Lyle said in a much stronger voice than he'd had before he left the room.

"She needs her rest right now."

"I want to find out about the test," Meghan shot back, berating herself for snapping at him. "I'm sorry. I just want to know what they found."

"Nurse said that we won't know until morning. So, you might as well go home. I'm doing fine. I don't need ya hovering over me, girlie. I just want to get some sleep."

Lyle's words cut like a knife, yet she knew he was concerned about her. "Are you sure? I can stay a while longer."

"Yes, I'm sure. Now, go on home. In the morning, you are going to need to make sure all is okay at the pharmacy. Someone needs to receive that delivery. Can you do that?"

"I'll take care of everything. Don't worry about it."

Lyle pointed a finger at Jake. "You make sure she gets home all right, young man."

"I will, sir. Hope you feel better."

"I'll feel just fine with some sleep. So, go on, get." He shooed them with a hand.

Before leaving the floor, Meghan stopped at the nurses' station. She scribbled down her number and handed it to a pretty redhead. "Call me at the slightest change in Lyle's condition."

"He's in good hands. Go home and get some rest."

She started for the elevators, Jake at her side. In the parking lot, he said, "I'll follow you home and make sure you get inside."

The trip to Brooksville was pure agony for Meghan. Leaving Lyle at the hospital didn't sit well but she knew he was being taken care of.

She drove down Main, still numb. She parked her

car in front of Lily's, a spark taking hold inside. Jake wasn't going to like it, but she was going with him to her house. Being with him made her feel secure and she yearned for that right now.

Purse in hand, she headed for his SUV, jumping into the passenger-side before he could say anything. He stared at her, not sure what was happening. "I'm going with you."

"Meghan, it's not safe for you to be with me right now."

"They don't know where you are, and I'll have Lily come pick me up in the morning."

He looked like he wanted to object but shoved the gearshift into drive. and took off, taking all the back streets out of town.

Meghan sat back and relaxed for the first time since she returned from getting food that afternoon. By the time they'd parked in the back of her home, she'd nodded out. When she opened her eyes, she found Jake carrying her through the back door and to her room where he gently placed her onto the bed.

"I'll sleep on the couch." He turned to leave.

"Please don't leave, Jake. Sleep here with me."

"Are you sure?"

"Yes."

She wasn't going to think about anything else. He was here with her and that's all that mattered.

Chapter Twenty-One

Jake removed his shirt and sat on the bed to pull off his boots. Meghan had gone to the bathroom and had left him to wonder what had changed to make her want to be with him. Was it all about what had happened that day—that she needed comfort, or did she care about him? He wished he knew which.

He laid back on the mattress, his arm tucked behind his head on the pillow, thinking it was best to let her make any moves. He wasn't forcing her to do anything she didn't want to.

The door opened and she stepped out in a blue T-shirt and a pair of light blue, checked, drawstring shorts, the sight of her legs causing his crotch to tighten. *Keep it together.* She didn't need him attacking her the minute she got into bed.

She rushed to get under the covers and pulled the blanket up to her chin. No way was that a come and get me, big boy response, and it instantly cooled his ardor.

"Are you okay, Meghan?"

She turned to look at him. "I'm worried about Lyle. Do you think he'll be okay?"

"He seemed all right when we left, and the hospital will call if anything changes. I'm sure he wouldn't want you to fuss over him. Would he?"

She shook her head. "I know he wouldn't, but it's hard not to."

Jake smiled, wanted to reassure her, though not knowing how. "You really love that old man, don't you?"

"More than anything. He's more like family than my own. He really cares about me, unlike my dad, who wanted to marry me off to someone who treats women like chattel."

"Yeah, why would your father do that to you?"

"Because Tom is a big man about town and has money to spare a drunk in need of some. Everything is a bartering tool to my father, and the church sanctions it all. That's why I got out and was safe until they found me. I want to thank you again for helping me get out from under their control. I don't know what I would have done otherwise."

"You would have figured something out but I'm glad I could help. A man like your ex-fiancé needs to be brought down a few pegs."

"Yes, and the church that created this male, dominating culture. We aren't living in the stone ages. Women are way past having men control them."

"Amen." Jake shifted onto his side, facing her.

She smiled, one that lit up her whole face.

His body revolted again. *Damn it all to hell.* This woman stirred a desire in him like no other. But this wasn't the time for that. She needed him for comfort, not to seduce her.

"We'd better get some sleep." He rolled onto his other side and reached out to turn the light off on the nightstand. It was going to be hard to rest. Yet he was going to have to try for her sake, especially since she needed to be at work early in the morning.

Minutes ticked by in agony for Jake and when he

was about to doze off, a loud bump jerked him alert. What was it? Was someone outside? Again?

Jake eased out of bed, trying hard not to wake Meghan who was asleep beside him.

He stepped out of the bedroom, catching sight of a figure passing by the window. *Shit.* Had Andrew or one of his henchmen found him. He never should have allowed Meghan to stay here with him. Now, she was in danger.

Slowly, he crept to the window and looked out, seeing an outline of a man standing next to the door. Was this guy going to try and break in?

With a sense of dread, he waited and watched, his breath catching in his chest, his heart racing a mile a minute.

A knock had him releasing the air in his lungs. No way was it someone who was there with bad intentions. They wouldn't knock on the door.

He walked over to switch on the porch light and looked out the side window. Cullen stood there blinking from the bright stream.

Jake quickly opened the door and allowed Cullen inside. "What are you doing here?"

"I heard through my back channels that you were right about something big that was about to happen. I checked into this farmer. Apparently, he's accrued a large amount of fertilizer, gone unchecked since he'd bought from some unscrupulous sources. You know what they use that shit for, right?"

"To build a bomb. How much are we talking about here? Enough to blow up a building or enough to blow a city block to smithereens?"

Cullen cleared his throat and said, "The latter."

"Christ. What are we going to do?"

"As we are speaking, Malaysia and a few others are on their way out to this farm to find out if the fertilizer is still there. Hopefully, we can stop this before anyone is put at risk. But if we can't, we are going to need every man on deck to find out what they plan to do."

"I'm here to help," Jake said with conviction. "What can I do?"

"You can put on a pot of coffee. We need to wait to hear from Malaysia. She said she'd call me when they found out anything."

"I'll start the coffee." Meghan's voice startled both men, especially Cullen who didn't know she was there. He looked at her, then Jake and frowned. "I thought you were alone."

Jake shrugged. "It is her home."

"I can be assured that what you just overheard will not leave this house?"

"Of course," Meghan said immediately. "You can trust me."

She left them to go to the kitchen. When she'd gone, Cullen gave him a sheepish grin. "You and Meghan, huh?"

Jake wasn't sure what to say. Were they together? Not really but he sure as hell wanted them to be. Maybe he should tell her how he felt and see what she had to say. At least he'd know where he stood. "I'm not sure what you'd call us."

"Don't waste time trying to figure it out. For years I danced around my feelings for Malaysia. We could have been together so much sooner if I hadn't. Don't waste precious time."

Jake nodded. Cullen was right. He'd talk to Meghan.

But not tonight. They had too much going on. He'd have that conversation when life and limb weren't at stake.

Meghan returned from the kitchen with two mugs of coffee in hand and handed one to Cullen and him the other.

"Hope black is okay?" She looked at Cullen. Meghan knew Jake took his black.

"Black is perfect. Thank you."

Jake took a sip of his, the aroma alone reviving him. "You're not going to have any?" he asked her when he noticed she hadn't gone back to get a cup for herself.

"Not right now." She fidgeted, and he wondered why.

Cullen's phone played a sing-song tone and he quickly answered. "Yep. Shit. Okay. Yeah, I'm here with Jake. I'll see you in a few."

The guy and the fertilizer are nowhere to be found. This ups the stakes a thousand percent. We have to find out where he is, and we need to do it pronto."

"How are we going to do that?" Jake's mind spun a mile a minute.

"I think I should go into the compound and see if Andrew is there," Cullen said deeply, worry lines now furrowed in his forehead.

"I'm going with you."

Cullen shook his head. "As far as I know, Andrew doesn't suspect me. You, though, I don't know."

"You, yourself, said that he stopped talking to you. That might be because he doesn't trust you. If we go together, we could at least have each other's backs."

Cullen scrubbed his beard. It was clear he was contemplating what Jake had said. "All right but we need to wait for Malaysia to get here. She can have our back

175

on the outside. We can be wired up and if things go wrong, she can get in to help."

"I'm not leaving Meghan here by herself. She has issues of her own. She needs my protection."

"I can take care of myself," Meghan shot back, her face now masked in anger.

"Not while Tom is in town. We can drop you off at Lily's before we go in."

She signed. "Okay. I have to be to work early for that delivery anyway. Also, I have to check on Lyle."

Jake knew if he asked her not to, she would disagree, so he didn't bother. Meghan had a mind of her own and he couldn't change that no matter how much he'd like to.

****

Meghan knew trying to sleep would be futile. She didn't want to admit it to herself, but she was frightened for Jake. Going into that compound was dangerous and he might not come back. The mere idea of losing him caused tears to cloud her vision. Why hadn't she told him not to go? Like he would have listened. Maybe if she'd have told him about his impending fatherhood, he might have had second thoughts.

Too late for should haves or what ifs. She just needed to pray he and Cullen got out alive. Cullen. Boy had that been a surprise. She never would have guessed the man was law enforcement. Not in a million years. Looks were deceiving in his case.

She paced Lily's kitchen, too pent up to sit still. She glanced at the clock on the wall, surprised it was getting close to daylight. She might as well go take a shower and get her butt down to the pharmacy. She could finish stocking before that delivery came. Without a pharmacist in house, she really couldn't stay open for anything other than what Lyle had filled and over-the-counter supplies, but she could get things ready for when they could fill prescriptions again.

Once she'd showered and dressed, she quickly took her prenatal vitamin and her anti-nausea pill and left the house, rechecking the door to make sure it was locked. Tom could be lurking about, and she didn't want her best friend in any danger.

Meghan raced to her car and locked the doors, nervous and apprehensive at being alone. She needed to make it to the pharmacy, set the alarm and lock herself in. The place was like a fortress once inside.

On Main Street, she started to worry about Jake again. She had his cell phone number in hers now, only a phone call away with what was going on, yet it left a bad feeling in her stomach.

Instead of parking in the back, she chose the front where the streetlights were on. She raced to unlock the door. Once inside, she relocked it and hurried to enter the alarm code. For now, she was safe. She prayed Jake was just as lucky.

She blew out a breath and walked to the back to turn on all the lights and get a box or two to restock the shelves. She had to stay busy, or she'd lose her mind.

When she was folding three boxes she'd finish emptying, a knock on the back door caused her to jump. She glanced up at the clock and noted it was nine already.

Had to be the delivery they'd been expecting. Thank God they had cameras in the back to make sure. She checked to see that it was indeed the delivery driver and went to let him in, quickly paid him with the check Lyle had filled out yesterday and relocked the door. With nothing else to do, she sat down in the backroom where she and her boss had lunch every day, his absence causing her to tear up again. Her heart hurt. What if he couldn't come back? What would she do? Would he have to sell the pharmacy? She'd be out of a job if he did. This was why he'd wanted her to go to school. So, she could take over for him. Was she even smart enough to do that? She didn't know and now with a baby on the way, was there even a possibility of that?

Her life was in turmoil right now.

One thing she should do was figure out what her feelings were for Jake. Being around him made her feel safe but was that all it was?

Her body tingled in his presence yet was it more than attraction? She wasn't sure. Why couldn't she get a handle on her feelings? She'd never been in love before, never cared enough about anyone since her childhood had been so fraught with disillusion and despair. She was afraid that she'd end up like her mother—scared to allow a man to take everything and give nothing back. Was Jake capable of that? Up until a few days ago, she hadn't even known his real name.

She inhaled a breath. What would Lyle think if he knew she and Jake were married? Would he be angry that she chose to do something so impulsive? All these questions were giving her a headache. It was time to put them away since she had to open the pharmacy for at least half the day.

She rose and walked to the front, glancing out at the street, a handful of people already milling around. She turned off the alarm and quickly unlocked the door and flipped over the closed sign.

Work right now would only help to keep her sane. No sooner had she made it back to the counter when the door signaled an entrance. Her jaw slackened when she saw that it was Mrs. Ferguson.

She headed straight for her, a paleness of her skin giving Meghan pause. The last time she saw her she was orange, now she looked like a ghost.

"Meghan," the older woman said, her breathlessness obvious.

Meghan immediately came around to meet the woman, reaching out to steady her when she swayed. "Come sit down, Mrs. Ferguson." She led her to a chair and helped her sit. "What seems to be the problem?"

"I visited the doctor a few days ago and he prescribed another drug for my blood pressure. I've been taking it, but he makes me feel terrible. Is Lyle around so I can ask him about this drug?"

"Lyle is in the hospital. Do you know what the drug is?"

"I brought the bottle." She reached in her handbag and handed Meghan the container of pills.

Meghan glanced at the name, having seen Lyle fill this drug many times. It could cause many side effects and could also alter her thyroid medication she knew the woman was taking.

"What time of day do you take these?" Meghan sat down beside her.

"I take all my pills in the morning."

Meghan frowned. "Can I suggest that you not do that? I know you take a prescription for your thyroid. You need to take that pill at least an hour before eating and four hours before any other drug for it to work correctly. Did they not tell you that at the other pharmacy?"

The old woman hung her head. "They don't like me

there. Lyle would talk to me about this stuff, and sometimes if I'm not reminded, I forget."

Meghan's gut clenched. Now she felt bad about what had happened with her. She needed guidance and felt awful about judging her too harshly.

She reached out and rubbed the woman's arm. "How about I write all this down for you so that you can revisit it when you get confused. Would that be all right?"

Mrs. Ferguson's face lit up. "That would be so kind of you, Meghan, and please tell Lyle I hope he gets better soon."

"I will. Let me quickly get a slip of paper and I'll write all that down." She went to get what she needed, thinking that this pharmacy staying open was important to the community. Lyle cared about the people he served, and if that meant her picking up the slack, she'd need to, no matter how hard it would be or how long it'd take.

Chapter Twenty-Two

Jake followed Cullen out of the compound, afraid to look back in case someone was aiming a gun at him. They'd gone in to find Andrew sitting behind his desk, appearing normal for all to see. Although he never did any of the dirty work himself, he expected other people to take the fall.

With angry eyes, he'd stared daggers at Jake, and if looks could have killed, he'd be a dead man right now. He knew Jake had been there under false pretenses.

He and Cullen were lucky they were still alive, but maybe Andrew knew there were people there to protect them if anything happened. He did have security around the compound. Maybe he'd spotted Malaysia and her crew and chose not to retaliate at this time, but that didn't mean he wouldn't. Both would need to watch their backs unless the guy ended up in jail. Even then, he probably had outreach.

"We need to find that damn farmer. He's getting ready to do something as we speak," Cullen said, drawing him out of his troubled thoughts.

"How are we going to do that? He could be anywhere."

"Malaysia is running a check on his vehicle registrations now. We'll put a bolo out on them and see if he isn't spotted. In the meantime, we need to figure out where they'd strike. Somewhere that would cause the most collateral damage and hit who they hate the most."

Jake scratched his head. "Do you have any ideas? I can't think of a thing."

"A synagogue or a mosque maybe."

"Maybe, but somehow, those don't feel flashy enough for the likes of Andrew. He'd want to do something huge, something on the Timothy McVeigh scale."

"Let's hope not." Cullen looked aghast. "We have to find this guy now."

Both men jumped into Jake's SUV and made a b-line for downtown. "

"Should we get the local police involved?" Cullen asked.

"I'm not sure if we can trust the sheriff. When I'd first heard about Kennett, Andrew had been concerned about Hanson questioning him, but that doesn't mean the sheriff isn't sympathetic to his cause. I, myself, tried to talk to him about the missing man. He told me that they had reason to believe he was in Canada. That seemed awful convenient. Whoa, wait a minute. Where did Kennett work? Planning and Zoning at the Municipal building, right? Could he have given Andrew something that caused him to disappear? Wouldn't they have all the schematics for buildings in the area? That would show all their weak points perhaps.

"By George, I think you might have something here. Let's go see. If we're lucky, we might find out what layout he looked at last because I believe that you must sign for everything you check out."

Jake took off for city hall. Planning and Zoning was directly behind that building. Now, they had something to go on until they heard from Malaysia and needed to work fast since lives were at stake.

Ten minutes later, he and Cullen were entering Planning and Zoning. With Cullen's authority, they should be able to excess what they needed. At the counter, Jake waited for Cullen to explain what they had to see and were quickly ushered back to where Kennett used to work and all the files they'd need to check.

"You take the computer," Cullen said. "I'll dig into this filing cabinet. It's got to be in one or the other."

Jake turned on the computer and typed in Kennett's name, finding the man's files. He quickly scanned the content, one date standing out, two days before the man disappeared. He opened the folder and noted a schematic. He pressed on it and up came a building plan. He glanced at the bottom and his throat went dry. "Cullen." Jake glanced over at him.

"Yeah, what?"

"I think I have something."

Cullen came over to look, his eyes instantly widening. "Why would they choose that facility?"

"It does house a lot of people of color," Jake said, a sick, sinking feeling forming in the pit of his stomach. "And they have families visiting on certain days. Shit, what day is it today?"

"Fuck!" Cullen reached in his jean's pocket for his cell phone. "I need to call Malaysia and get her to contact the prison. They need to be looking for any strange vehicles in the parking lot. Anything capable of containing a bomb."

Jake closed the files and rose, waiting for Cullen to relay everything to her as they started out the door. "You don't think this could be a possible prison break, could it? Do you know if Andrew had any family or friends in that facility?"

Cullen held the door open, and Jake stepped outside, noting the sky had turned dark. A storm was coming, and it only made him more on edge.

In the vehicle, Jake set his GPS for the prison and raced out of town. They were going to run straight into the storm that was brewing. One intense minute led to ten and they were bucking a strong wind, rain now pelting his windshield, the wipers barely keep up. It was becoming difficult to keep his SUV on the road. "This is getting bad, find a weather station and see what they're saying."

Cullen switched on the radio, static crackling through talk and music. "Beep...beep...beep. This is the National weather service. A tornado warning has been issued for the counties over Warren, Jefferson, and Gasconade until eleven P.M. A twister was sited three miles southeast of Brookville, moving at five miles an hour. If you have a basement, you need to go there now, otherwise find an interior room of your home with no windows," an automated voice said.

"What a great time for this shit." Jake swerved to miss a limb that had come down in the roadway. "Take the next right." Cullen pointed to a turnoff ahead. "We may have to lay low until this storm passes."

Jake checked his GPS and saw they were still a good fifteen miles from the prison. He only had seconds to decide what was more important. "I'm going to keep going."

Cullen blew out a breath and nodded. "You're right. We are running out of time."

Jake gripped the steering wheel tight and drove past the turn, his thoughts ricocheting back to Meghan.

Hopefully, she was safe wherever she was, and would stay that way. All this danger had fomented something for him. He cared deeply for her and when he saw her next, he was going to tell her how much.

****

Meghan stepped out of the pharmacy and had to clutch her handbag to her side to keep it from blowing away. The wind was intense, the rain drenching her as she raced to the car, stopping long enough to retrieve her keys. A hand cupped her shoulder and she turned to find Andrew standing behind her, a look of concern on his face. Just him being near her caused the hairs on the back of her neck to charge. "What are you doing here?" she asked, her mind racing a mile and a half.

"You need to come with me."

By the tone of his voice, Meghan knew it wasn't a request but a command. What was she going to do? With what she'd learned that morning, no one was safe around this guy.

"I can't. I must get to the hospital." She hoped that knowledge would change things somehow.

He grasped her arm. "The hospital will have to wait."

Meghan wanted to scream, but over the gale force wind, no one would hear her, especially since it looked as if the streets were deserted.

She was forced to get into his car from the driver's door and he slid in beside her, speeding off in the direction of the compound. What did he want with her?

He turned into the parking area at the front entrance and dragged her from the car.

"Let go of me." She tried hard to get loose.

"Do you want me to hurt you?" he said, his eyes

fierce.

Meghan swallowed hard and allowed him to pull her inside the building, the coldness of the place and people chilling her to the bone. It didn't help that she was soaked to the skin. He led her down a long, narrow hallway to an office.

"Sit down," he said, closing and locking the door.

Meghan bit her bottom lip. What was he going to do to her? She didn't even want to think about it.

She shuffled over to the chair in front of the desk and eased down, refusing to look at the man. She was afraid of what she'd see. All these supremacists seemed to have no respect for the female race. Look what Felix had tried to do to her. Would Andrew do the same? The mere idea made her nauseous, almost to the point of retching in her mouth.

The creaking of the chair across from her signaled he'd taken a seat. "Your boyfriend got a cell phone number?"

Meghan glanced up, coming to the realization that she was here for the soul purpose of luring Jake back to the compound. She wasn't going to help him—ever.

"I don't have a boyfriend." It wasn't a lie. Jake was her husband, but Andrew would never find that out from her.

"I'd hate to hurt you, blondie, but I will if I have to."

The threat was real. She saw it in the depths of his eyes. But she still wasn't going to tell him. She cared more for Jake than for her own safety.

"Who are you talking about?"

Andrew rose, came around the desk, snatched her purse from her hand and dumped the contents onto the desktop. He reached for her phone as he went back to sit down, a moment later snarling at her. "Passcode," he snapped.

"Seven, eight, three, two." She prayed that he hadn't figured out that Jackson wasn't Jake's real name.

He thumbed through her stuff, and looked up at her, his eyes darker than before. "Where the fuck is Jackson's number?"

"Why would I have Jackson's number?" It was easy to lie to him since Jackson Gallagher wasn't a real person, but a persona Jake had created.

He growled and threw her phone on the desk, his attention diverted to the pill bottles.

Great. Would he be able to figure out what they were for? Probably. He examined the medication, looked at her and smiled. "You and Jackson are expecting, huh?"

Meghan refused to answer. The truth would only help Andrew and she wasn't going to do that. He could believe what he wanted. She wasn't going to confirm it.

"Cat got your tongue?"

She stared at him, refusing to be goaded. He rose and started to pace the room, his fists clenched at his side. When he stopped, Meghan held her breath, waiting to see what he was going to do. He reached for her phone again and punched in something and waited. "Where are you, Meghan?" she heard her best friend ask.

What was Andrew planning?

"Lily, this is Andrew Gibson. I have Meghan here at the compound. I want you to tell Jackson if he wants her safely returned, he'd better show up here. Do you understand?"

He ended the call and went to sit down, leaning back in his chair, smiling at her. "Now, we wait and see how

187

much you matter to him. If he shows, he cares. If he doesn't, I guess you'll know where you stand."

Meghan wanted to deny the man's claims, but she had no idea how Jake felt about her. Right now, that didn't matter. She didn't want him placed at risk to prove that one way or the other.

Chapter Twenty-Three

Jake glanced ahead, relieved they'd made it to the prison gates. The storm had slowed them down a lot, made them pull under an overpass to keep from being sucked up by a twister that has come close. He prayed Meghan was somewhere safe.

He drove up to the security office and Cullen handed the man his badge and they were quickly ushered inside the gates. Jake sped up to the parking area, both he and Cullen looking for a vehicle able to hold explosives. Five security officers were already checking the lot, examining possible trucks. They both jumped out of his SUV and went over to help. They might have only minutes to locate the device before it went off.

Jake ran through a row of smaller cars, thinking they weren't a possibility. A vehicle off to the side of the building drew his attention. "Cullen," he hollered, pointing to a black king cab dully with a camper shell on the back.

His friend nodded and they both headed for the truck, Jake's heart ratcheting in his chest. Cullen looked in the back window, his eyes widening. "This is it. I see a timer. Looks like it's going to go off in eleven minutes."

Jake sucked in a breath. If they would've stopped any longer, they never would have made it here in time. "Do you have any experience with disarming a bomb?"

Jake asked Cullen.

"Yes. I want everyone to get back. See if one of the officers inside can't get everyone near that wall away just in case something goes wrong."

Shit. Way to make a man feel insecure about those abilities.

He raced to tell the officers and returned to Cullen. He planned to stay here. If Cullen went boom, so would he.

Slowly, Cullen opened the hatch on the camper and eased his way inside. Jake could now hear a slight tick, no doubt the countdown to blast. While it was ticking, he'd be breathing.

Time seemed to stand still as every muscle in Jake's body tensed. What if Cullen couldn't discharge it? He wouldn't be able to say goodbye to Meghan. Tell her how much he cared about her. For such a short period of time of knowing someone, he couldn't believe how much she meant to him—hell, he loved her. He knew that now since he was facing his possible demise. If he made it out of here alive, he was going to tell her that.

He glanced back at Cullen who had taken a pocketknife out of his jeans and was separating four wires, his hands steady for a man about to die. The guy had nerves of steel. The clock now read nine minutes.

He had nine minutes to live. What could he do in that time. Praying seemed like a good option. If Cullen didn't cut the right wire, it could be all over.

Jake squeezed his eyes closed.

Imagines of his family popped into his head, his niece, nephews, his sister, his mother, and finally his beautiful Meghan, someone he wanted all his loved ones to meet. She was his wife and if he lived, he was going to make sure she stayed his wife.

The ticking stopped. Was this the end?

Jake held his breath for impact. Nothing happened.

He opened his eyes to see Cullen leaning back against the truck, a yellow wire in the bomb cut.

The air in his chest came rushing out. The clock on the face of the bomb had stopped at exactly five minutes.

He helped Cullen out of the camper and shook the man's hand. No way could Jake have done what Cullen had. They turned and walked toward the front of the prison right as two vehicles pulled in through the gates. Malaysia jumped out and ran toward Cullen. "Did you find it?"

"It's been disarmed." She ran into his arms and held him tight.

This was Jake's cue to leave. He needed to find Meghan and tell her he loved her.

"If you don't mind, I'm going to take off. I got to see a girl about some feelings I need to reveal."

Cullen clapped him on the arm. "You do that, and I'll see you later."

Jake nodded, heading for his SUV. The storm above had passed, the sun's rays were now trying to peek through the clouds. It was like what they'd just gone through. The sunshine after the darkness.

He grabbed his cell phone and pressed Meghan's number. It rang and rang. Why wasn't she answering. He'd call Lily. He quickly located her contact info and pressed call.

"Jackson, where are you?"

"I'm on my way back from Amherst prison. Do you know where Meghan is?"

"Andrew Gibson has her at the compound. He said

to tell you that he'll be expecting you."

"Shit." So much for that ray of hope he'd had moments ago. It had just blown up in his face.

He had to get to Meghan before any harm came to her. She'd become his world, and he wasn't going to allow anyone, especially Andrew, to take that away.

He sped up, having to dodge tree limbs all the way back to Brooksville. He slowed down in town, afraid he'd be stopped for speeding. At the compound, the adrenaline that had kept him going left his body. *Damn it.* He needed it now more than ever. Somehow, he had to get Meghan to safety. That was paramount in his mind.

He walked to the door and stepped inside, the quiet instantly unnerving him. Jake went straight for Andrew's office. The door was closed and that only worried him more. He never closed it. Andrew better not have touched one hair of Meghan's head. Not one single strand or he'd strangle him.

He pushed the door open and walked inside, Meghan's face instantly changing from calm to frightened. Andrew was sitting behind his desk, looking smug, too cool for Jake's liking.

"It's about time, Gallagher. I was starting to wonder if you'd decided she wasn't worth risking your life."

"You better not have touched her, Gibson."

The man smiled. "She's not my type, especially now that she's got a baby onboard."

Jake's head snapped back to Meghan who looked even more frightened. "What is he talking about?"

"Oh, so he didn't know, Meghan? You bad, bad girl, you."

"Meghan?" Jake stared at her, suddenly realizing why she'd looked so pale and sickly. "Are you pregnant?"

She didn't say a word, just nodded. This revelation upped the stakes a hundred percent. They were going to have a child and getting her safely out of here, without causing her any pain, had to be the goal, even if it meant dying for her. His family would take care of her—he knew that with certainty. She needed to know that.

"Listen to me, Meghan, if anything happens to me, I need you to tell my family who you are. They will help you with the baby."

Andrew's calm expression vanished, and he scowled. "I thought you didn't have family. You said you were raised in foster homes."

"I lied."

"I'm going to kill the person who vetted you."

"I hope you do. There'll be one less asshole in the world." Jake was goading the man, but if he was going to die, he was going to make sure the man knew how much he despised his kind. That hating people for being different was *evil* and no one should tolerate it.

****

Meghan couldn't believe that Jake was being so glib with Andrew. It was almost as if he was trying to anger him. She didn't understand. But men were foreign to her in so many ways. What she hadn't expected was for him to say that his family would help her raise their child if anything were to happen to him. That blew her mind. It was clear he had an upbringing different to her own. Yes, her mother had cared for her, yet not enough to get out of an abusive relationship and make her daughter's life better. That spoke volumes to Meghan.

"What do you want from me, Andrew?" Jake's question drew her back to him.

"Right now, I want to know who they hell you are."

"Nobody important. Now, are you going to let Meghan go? She has no part in this."

"Oh, but she does because she's someone who means something to you."

"Just fucking let her go."

The man's eyes narrowed. "You don't *fucking* tell me what I can and cannot do, Gallagher, or is that even you name?"

Jake shrugged. "Does that really matter?"

Andrew sneered, shifting in his chair, agitated by Jake's cavalier attitude. He expected something different and that only made Meghan more nervous. Maybe Jake needed to be a little less irritating to the guy?

"Where's Cullen?" Andrew asked, his gaze trained on Jake. He knew somehow the two were not who they seemed.

"He's your sidekick. Shouldn't you know that?"

"I think we both know that's not true. What about you, Meghan? Did you know the man was a plant? Or have they left you in the dark?"

"I don't know anything," she said. Sure, she was lying, but this man was evil, and she wasn't going to say anything that could jeopardize anyone's life.

"While we're in this question-and-answer phase, Andrew, where is Kennett? He helped you out with schematics for the prison and you repaid his kindness by murdering him. Where'd you hide the body?"

Meghan sucked in a ragged breath, her attention darting from one man to the other. She couldn't believe Jake was being so brazen when they were both at the mercy of the man sitting across from them.

Andrew's features changed. He'd seemed mildly

annoyed before. Now, he was furious.

"What do you know about the prison?" Andrew asked in a tone that scared Meghan.

"I know that a farmer friend of yours placed a bomb outside the building—one that was disarmed about forty-five minutes ago. I'm sure law enforcement have him in custody by now and is questioning him as to your involvement. Other than that, nothing," Jake said.

Meghan held her breath. This wasn't going to end well for any of them. She glanced at the door, wondering if she could make it there and out of the building before shots were fired. Probably not.

Sirens echoed in the distance, ones that instantly drew Andrew's attention. He went for the top drawer of his desk, but before he could get it open, Jake flew over the top and pushed him back. The two rolled onto the floor, swinging at one another, each trying to get in a hard punch.

Meghan didn't know what to do. If she tried to intervene, she could harm the child growing inside her. Knowing that, she was forced to watch, feeling helpless.

Andrew pulled a knife from his boot, and she screamed, so loud it pierced her eardrums.

Moments later, Cullen, Malaysia and three other men with black jackets rushed into the room and grabbed ahold of Andrews arm right before he was able to stab Jake in the chest. The look on the man's face when he realized it was Cullen cuffing him appeared deadly.

"Fuck you, asshole," he said to Cullen right before the other men pushed him out of the room.

"Was it something I did?" Cullen asked, laughing.

Every nerve in Meghan's body recoiled. How close had they come to dying? They'd never know.

Jake walked over to her and pulled her into his arms. His touch made her relax. He was the only person to ever make her feel safe and that had to mean something. Actually, it meant a lot, and she knew with certainty that she loved him. She just prayed he felt the same.

Chapter Twenty-Four

Jake sat waiting for Cullen to finish up his interrogation with Andrew after giving his own statement to the police. Meghan was now in with the sheriff. If nothing else, they could get Gibson on kidnapping charges.

When she finished, he was going to tell her how he felt—that he loved her and wanted to stay married. That having a child with her would be a high point in his life and he was looking forward to a bright future together. If she would have him.

Cullen stepped out the door and smiled at Jake. "We got him, and his men because of those guns you told us about. Stolen, of course. As we speak, the local officers are searching the woods outside town for Kennett's body. Apparently, he got cold feet about what they'd planned to do, and Andrew did his own dirty work in this case and killed him and one of his men murdered Bruce Severs, the Farmers Insurance agent, who got suckered into the plan later and wanted out. Andrew confessed to it all and now we have him on kidnapping and murder. He's going to spend the rest of his life in prison."

Jake blew a relieved breath. They were going to pay, and he was happy to be a part of it. "It couldn't have happened to a more deserving guy. What about Rim and his buddy? How much time do you think they'll spend in jail?"

"A minimum of five to seven years. I wouldn't worry about them for quite a while."

"That's good to hear. What's next for you?"

"I'm taking a few months off. Going to propose to my lady and spend the next few weeks just being with her. What about you?"

"I'm going to convince Meghan to stay married and try to rebuild my reputation as a right-side-of-this-issue journalist."

"Let me help you with that." Cullen slapped him on the back. "Bringing down a notorious White Supremacist should do the trick. Your name will be mentioned when this all comes out, and with you and Meghan testifying against the man, you should have everything cleared up."

"I appreciate that, Cullen, and if I can ever return the favor, you know where to find me."

"Actually, I don't."

"I'll be here. I'm not leaving Meghan and I know she loves Lyle Strom too much to leave him. There is a local paper I can try to get on. Until then, I'll dig ditches if I have to, to stay."

"That sounds like a plan. Now, I got to run out to the compound. Malaysia and her crew are still out there searching the place. Who knows what else they'll uncover."

"Take care of yourself, Cullen."

"You do the same."

Jake watched him leave, turning back to wait for Meghan. He was too antsy to sit down, so instead, he paced the hall. Once everything was settled with her, he'd call his family and let them know what he'd been doing. He didn't want them to not have a heads-up when the story broke. Too bad he couldn't write it himself. But he was too close to it, and that would seem opportunistic to do so. Though, he could write a book, something he'd wanted to do for a long time. This could be a perfect opportunity to start.

A door opened and he turned to find Meghan and the sheriff stepping out. She saw Jake and smiled.

He rushed to her. "Is everything okay?"

"Yeah, I'm just tired, and a little shaky since I haven't eaten since breakfast."

"Well, let's go get you something to eat and we can talk."

Outside, he held her hand, led her to his SUV and helped her inside. Once he was behind the wheel, he looked at her. "What do you feel like?"

"I don't care. You choose."

He started the engine, pulled out of the police parking lot and headed for the diner out on the outskirts of town. A few minutes later, they were headed inside.

Meghan stopped halfway down the aisle, Jake almost colliding with her back. She stood staring at the guy Jake had met the last time he was at the diner. How did Meghan know him?

"Why haven't you left town yet?" she said in a tone Jake hadn't heard her use before. There was hate in her voice, but why?

The man sitting in the booth smiled up at Jake, amusement playing over his features. Suddenly, her words sank in. This was the guy she was supposed to marry, the one her father admired. He studied the man, nothing striking standing out. He seemed pretty mediocre to Jake. Had he known who Jake was when he'd met him, or was he surprised by who Meghan married? Only one way to find out. Ask.

"I assumed you're Tom Harkin?" he said, not really expecting an answer. He knew who he was. He didn't have to confirm it.

"And you must be my ex's new husband, right? Jake something or other."

Jake didn't answer, just glared at the man. He had no respect for a guy who'd force a woman into a marriage she didn't want. Most despicable thing he'd ever heard. Her father was equally appalling. That was a given, and he planned to tell him that if he ever saw him again.

"Why are you still here, Tom?" Meghan's question drew Jake back to her.

"Don't get your panties in a wad, Meg. I'm leaving. I just stopped to eat first. I have my pick of women. I'm not planning to wallow."

She huffed and started down the aisle to a booth in the far back. She slid into the seat, her cheeks looking flushed. He sat across from her, wanting to be next to her but thinking that would be too presumptuous. She was already upset. He didn't want to add to that.

"You okay?"

"Yeah. I just didn't expect to see him here."

"Hopefully, you'll never have to again."

She picked up the menu from the condiment stand against the window, her shaky hands giving away so much. If Jake could take away her anger, he'd do it.

A waitress came over, took their order and left. Now it was time for some serious talk. He just prayed it ended the way he wanted it to.

****

"Are you doing okay," he asked her again, reaching

out to squeeze her arm that rested on the table. Seeing Tom only made her angrier and she needed to calm down before it affected her stomach. She had enough problems right now with that. Her phone in her purse chirped and she reached in to check the message. *Oh, crap.* She forgot all about the doctor's appointment she had in an hour and unfortunately, it was too late to cancel it.

"We are going to have to eat fast. I have to be somewhere in an hour." Her announcement seemed to trouble Jake. But why?

The waitress brought their food, and she settled in to try and eat as least some.

"Where do you have to be?" he asked after he swallowed a bite of his burger.

She figured he might as well know the truth since he had everything to do with him. "I have a doctor's appointment to confirm my condition."

"Can I come with you?"

"Look, Jake, I don't expect you to be a part of this. I know you have a life somewhere else, and that you were only here to get a story."

He turned away, his jaw clenching. Was he upset with her? She wished she knew.

Jake looked back at her, his features unreadable. "We're married, Meghan. I want to share this with you if you'll let me."

"Why? You can't tell me this hasn't thrown you off? That you wanted this?"

"Probably no more than it did you. Sometimes life throws you curves, and things change."

"What are you saying? That you are excited by this? That you want to have a child with me?" She held the breath in her chest, waiting to hear his answer.

"Yes," he said without hesitation.

She released the air in her lungs, surprised by his response. "Are you sure?" Was she trying to talk him out of it? It sounded like it.

"I'm sure. When Andrew had you, I realized how much you meant to me. I know we haven't known each other for a long time but I love you, Meghan, and I want to be a part of your life. Will you let me?"

She swallowed hard, emotion clogging her throat. He'd said everything she'd wanted to hear, but could she trust it was because of her and not because of her being pregnant?

"It's okay if you don't feel the same. I'm not going to force anything on you."

She couldn't have asked for a better reply. He wanted her and he wasn't expecting anything. What more could she ask for.

Meghan glanced down at her phone. She needed to get going or she was not going to be on time. She took one last bite of her chicken sandwich, then wiped her face. "We'd better get going if we don't want to be late." She smiled. Hopefully, she didn't have to say it out loud. She wanted him to be there when she learned she was going to be a mother.

He nodded, paid the bill and they returned to his SUV. "Where is your doctor's office?" he asked when he was behind the wheel.

"On Main Street next to Commerce Bank."

He pulled out and they rode in silence.

Meghan didn't tell him she loved him, but she would. Right now, she was too nervous about her appointment. The next hour would make everything real. She was certain she was pregnant. This would just confirm it.

In the office, she and Jake sat quietly, another couple sitting across from them, married from the rock on the woman's finger.

Meghan's name was called. She reached for Jake's hand, and they were led back, and she was asked to give a urine sample and brought to a room. Fifteen minutes later, the doctor arrived and confirmed her condition. "It's early but we may be able to see something in a sonogram." He pulled a machine over and asked her to lie down and undo her jeans. He squeezed a clear gel over her belly. An image came up and he pointed to an area. "That's your baby." He moved over the dot and homed in, taking a picture and handing it to her.

She turned to Jake whose face seemed to have lit up. He really was happy about this. He held her hand tightly. This might have been something that neither had expected but they both wanted now and that was going to get them through the next eight months. Meghan loved Jake and she wanted him here with her and that's all that mattered. Everything else could be worked out as long as they were together.

A word about the author…

Jerri Drennen is an author of romantic suspense as well as paranormal and contemporary romance. Growing up on a farm in a tiny town in Minnesota was where she started reading romance and learned how to make up stories in her head. After meeting her husband, she moved to his hometown in Missouri where she now live with one of their four children. Her kids call her the crazy cat lady.

Thank you for purchasing
this publication of The Wild Rose Press, Inc.

For questions or more information
contact us at
info@thewildrosepress.com.

The Wild Rose Press, Inc.
www.thewildrosepress.com